BOOK 1

PROJECT BLACK BEAM

STEPHON FOWLKES

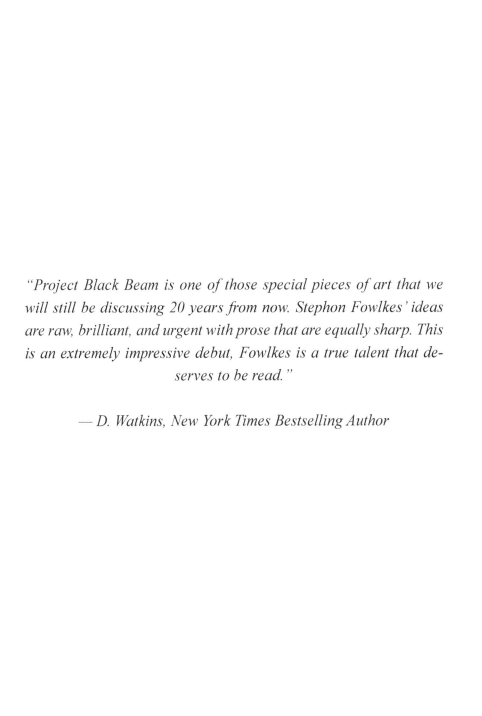

"Project Black Beam is one of those special pieces of art that we will still be discussing 20 years from now. Stephon Fowlkes' ideas are raw, brilliant, and urgent with prose that are equally sharp. This is an extremely impressive debut, Fowlkes is a true talent that deserves to be read."

— D. Watkins, New York Times Bestselling Author

Note to the Reader

The person who shared this book with you I consider them to be family. Love them to the best of your ability. I value them as much as I now value you.

Author Bio

Baltimore native, Stephon A. Fowlkes was born and raised in a historically underserved community on the west side of Baltimore with a vision to change the world with his creativity and expression. He has always been gifted in music and theater. With the support of his parents, he started his musical journey playing trumpet in elementary school at the age of 7. He played trumpet in the city's only elementary school jazz band at the time, under the direction of Mr James Pope, winning competitions and expressing himself through music in venues across the city. These experiences proved to be vital because he later used his gifts to audition and gain admittance into the Baltimore School for the Arts which helped to expand his network and creative prowess. While there, he expressed his passion for music as well as football. For him, the trumpet and theater were hobbies, and football was his dream. He departed from the school for the arts his senior year to follow his dream of football at his local high school Frederick Douglass Senior High School.

Stephon was born with metatarsus adductus but as an infant his father was persistent in applying braces to realign the bones in his legs. Many years later Stephon was named offensive MVP in his only year playing for his high school football team as a wide receiver and continued to play in college. He attended Coppin State University and played football there becoming a two-time National Champion and All-American honor recipient. This is when he released his first self-produced mixtape "Westside Story" under the moniker "IMP BEATZ". He saw the possibility of serving the community with his creativity, so he joined the same fraternity as his father, Iota Phi Theta, to continue the service and commitment instilled in him. He retained his love for music, creativity, and expression through the years making beats and performing. As a young adult, full-time college student, and independent artist working 2 jobs, he would endure financial hardship and a crippling environment despite his best efforts to overcome them. As a result, in 2017 he decided to serve his country and join the United States Army for stability and financial support as he strived to make his dreams a reality. While active, he graduated from infantry boot camp at Fort Leonard Wood, Missouri, and intelligence school in Fort Huachuca, Arizona. While serving he was involved in sensitive military programs that required the highest level of clearance and expertise. He returned to school to finish his Bachelor of Science in African American History and was invited to the National Society of Leadership and Success, the nation's largest honor society. Proving that he could do both service and music simultaneously, Stephon served honorably as an intelligence analyst and with multiple high-achieving medals and won a 3 round DMV radio contest. Stephon has written and performed as a local Hip Hop artist under the moniker "Locus" inspiring fans worldwide, opening for artists like French Montana, Meek Mill, Lil Durk, Miguel, Freeway, and others. While completing Project Black Beam he returned to Baltimore to work with alternatively placed youth as a mentor for the non-profit organization Lead4life. While his story is not over yet, it truly depicts passion, service, creativity, and resilience.

Acknowledgments

Writing this book has been equally more difficult and rewarding than I had imagined. I would not have been able to finish without my close friends and family, my mother and sisters being the first to hear the book's idea. Watching my mother's and younger sister's cheeks light up with delight made me feel loved and heard. My eternal thanks must be communicated to them for this. My parents, Angela and Joseph Fowlkes, instilled in me the qualities of humility and relying on God. They have never tried to steer me in a different direction. They were understanding and supportive when I left Baltimore to join the military to improve my financial condition so that I could follow my dreams.

I also want to express profound appreciation to my older sister Jazzmen for rebelliously acquiring a taste for rap music as a teen which in result exposed me to an exquisite catalog of the mid-90s — early 2000s rap music in my youth and for taking me to my first rap concerts. I want to express my heartfelt gratitude to my editor, Destinii Williams, who so diligently went through the manuscript with love and helped to polish the book to perfection.

I want to thank Sergeant Michael Hayes who was one of the only leaders of the Army that looked like me in the intelligence community. He showed up every day with a beautiful attitude and consistently taught and displayed how to exceed the military standard. To the individuals I grew up with, both those who made it to adulthood and those who did not, and to those who wanted nothing more than to enjoy the simple pleasures of life—You mean everything to me.

I want to thank my extended Iota Phi Theta family. The relationships I built there continue to prove absolutely priceless...I want to especially thank my brother Rodrick Johnson who consistently represents Black excellence in life as a man and as an educator. Thank you for being there for me in times I didn't know I needed. God has truly ordered our steps. I want to express my appreciation to everyone at Lead4life who work diligently to assist the youth who rely on them for every facet of life and for allowing me to work for such an amazing company.

To my family. To the late Grandma Jean and Grandma Mary. To Aunt Robin, Aunt Andrea, Pammie, Donya, Tommy, Skipper, Angelo, Joey, and Guy. Thank you for your prayers and for being a light to me.

Finally, a thank you to those I met along the way who may have unknowingly supported or inspired me during the development of this book and ultimately helped be apart of the village that brought this to fruition: Marquieta "Auntie" Hearn, Lennox Davis, Dominic "Smiley" Andrews, Joni King Jackson, Quentin Shaw, Shod Enterprises, "Zeus Supreme", Jarvis Staten, Rayana A. Young, Daichelle Lovejoy, Bro. "Thaddeus" Brower, D. Watkins, Joshua Jones, The Moorish Gates of Baltimore, Silent Books Publishing, Supreme Lifestyle, Brandon Burke, Blackwater Studios, Black Cat Studios, R.A.M.P, my professors at Coppin State University, and many many others.

Most of all, I thank God, because without God none of this would be possible.

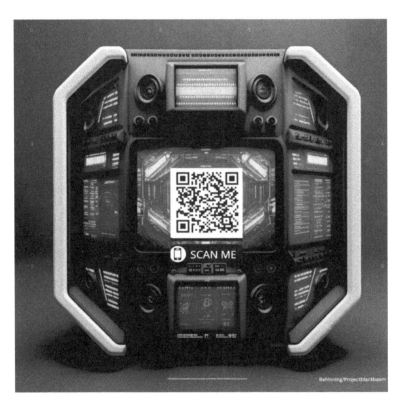

SCAN FOR MORE CONTENT AND TO UNLOCK ADDITIONAL
CHAPTERS

1. *Melanin (/ˈmɛlənɪn/; from Greek: μέλας melas)*
- A dark brown to black pigment occurring in the hair, skin, and iris of the eye in people. It is responsible for tanning of skin exposed to light. It is responsible for black not cracking and for the magic in black or the newly coined "melanated" girls and boys.

WINTER 2095:

Due to the impending extinction of melanated people, the U.S. government had decided to implement what was at the time deemed to be it's greatest resolution: *A federal mandate of every Black male born to immediately undergo surgical augmentation as a means of "protection and self-preservation."* The combination of man and machine. At the Beginning of the 21st century, scientists were mystified by the electronic properties that existed in melanin. They discovered that melanin has the incredible ability to transfuse and manipulate electronic/photon energy-unlike any other pigment and very few minerals. Engineers first began using melanin in computer chips, but their latest proposition is unlike any other.

This is Project Black Beam.

NEWS REPORT

"Lockhart Williams released a statement this morning stating they have successfully stabilized a 36% mortality rate during their cybertronic transhuman procedures. That's right, the stuff straight out of your favorite Science Fiction novel is finally here. Lockhart Williams corporation says they believe giving Blacks mechanized attributes and abilities (augmentation) will provide them a much-needed chance of survival and eventually a thriving lifestyle. They go on record assuring the federal government and it's people that they are fully allocating all available resources to reduce any risks associated with the procedure. Federal lawmakers have unanimously voted in favor of mandating what some are calling the weaponizing of all newborn Black males. The law is set to take place immediately and there are mixed emotions about it."

"A man without knowledge of himself and his heritage is like
a tree without roots."
-Dick Gregory

0.
PROLOGUE

The current year is 2108, and the military grade weapons developed nowadays can put a hole through a dime on the moon. No, that's an exaggeration, but the business of killing is still booming. It's been half a decade since society's candidates have decided that private gun ownership should be almost completely outlawed. Still it is common for the last people you'd trust with a gun to have primary access to them. Besides uniforms, the police force today aren't any different from the military and they'll put a hole in you quicker than a teenage girl with a blood fetish working summers at Claire's. Seriously, because they've been doing just that to us since the Rapture. Rules of engagement authorized deadly force to maintain total compliance to law, so we do whatever we can to avoid them.

Pay close attention, extremely pivotal things may only be mentioned once. From the early 2030s into the late 2060s White supremacists targeted electrical substations that serviced primarily Black neighborhoods and used the blackouts as opportunities for militias and small arms squads to carry out domestic terror attacks. Meanwhile, public health care in the United States would continue to decline, already ranked last on the list of developed countries as early as the year 2022. The cost of living and medical expenses continued to rise, the middle class shrank, and the wealth gap swelled.

Planning Parenting facilities continued to provide controversial contraceptive injections and abortions as solutions for low-income households who felt they lacked the adequate resources to deliver and or sufficiently raise their families.

Unfortunate circumstances and man-made pathogens made seeing a pregnant melanated woman a rare occurrence. Lack of an adequate diet and domestic terror attacks on food distribution centers created food deserts where illness and famine bred, a direct cause of many of our people being incapable of reproduction. It was common for decades to go by while entire cities remained absent of a Black child's presence.

In the year 2058, the *Rapture* had disproportionately targeted our people and it would not take long for our numbers to dwindle to a state of emergency. A world without melanated people is on the brink of existence, *"The birth of a new world"* they call it. Suicidal tendencies became common among our people. The inability to conceive and the coincidentally timed widespread occurrence of stillborn babies would drive many Blacks into a depressive state of mind. Mental health facilities exist but only for the well-off leaving poor women absent of professional input while accepting a life without their God-given gift of motherhood. Childbearing has become a privilege only the wealthiest and more stable Blacks could afford. The Rapture separated the country into what we now know as the up upper and lower wards. The lower wards are where the majority of surviving Blacks live and the upper wards are where a relatively puny number of Blacks and the rest of the exceptionally privileged people are allowed to live. Even in the most favorable of circumstances those "privileged" children grow accustomed to adopting a culture outside their own and being fed a feel-good curriculum which excludes us. Black children grow up having no accurate identity. These children will never speak in their true original tongues nor will they seek to. Their spirituality is rooted in outside influence. Their Gods won't look like them. Religions given to them will rob them of their ability to think critically. They know not of their true ancestral homeland or family. They have no leaders, irrigate, own very little land, acquire relatively 0 means of international travel outside the commercial industry, and possess no globally sufficient means of protecting their community's interests. They know not who they are and are left to adopt their divine sense of purpose from greed driven men who descend from the very colonizers who originally intended the lowliest of plights for our people. Adults continue to send their children to schools mandated by the government that exclude melanated people's contribution to modern society from the curriculum, leaving us and other minorities like us with a belittled disposition. They orientate us into society by carefully molding our minds for 13+ years of training and mis-education that further separates us from essential analytical and divergent thoughts. In these institutions we foster self-hate that we must overcome if we expect to create structure and overall internal stability.

For centuries powerful men in suits and ties have gathered and quarreled over how to spend profits made from the degradation and control of Black lives long before they are born. Men who historically have consistently looked to profit off us like cattle: from chattel slavery, the prison industry, fast food, music, alcohol, name brands etc. until present day. These men have understood that Black people could be subjugated and made servile by limiting their consciousness These are men who understand human consciousness co-creates reality.

Weapon manufacturers like Lockhart Williams Corporation use the natural phasing out of the Black race, which is now socially accepted, as an excuse to have our children as guinea pigs to further their trans-human/augmentee agenda and profit from verminous lucrative government contracts. Black children stripped from their mothers at birth and converted into weapons in labs in the name of "our protection."

HOW DID THIS REALITY COME ABOUT?

1.

Rap music at one point during the 21st century had begun to re-semble it's more powerful and spiritual self. Most rappers whose names rose to the surface of stardom throughout history had, believe it or not, barely scraped the edge of mastering this deeply complex art form. The greatest of us know that with the proper commitment to the sincerity of our words, coupled with the right timing and key, any person could do what many would consider humanly impossible. One could grow an entire forest or erect skyscrapers to cover every inch of the Earth however many times he or she pleased, and spawn it all from a rap. Yes! You read that correctly. We have the power to create life or death in abundance using our tongue and I want to be clear that I don't mean that figuratively. Rap was developing a codependent relationship with health and religion. Your doctor and your preacher both rap. The music was capable of truly healing and preventing epidemics. With the right cadence and mantra, we healed blindness and various diseases. You will witness it for yourself. What may seem like an urban legend or "Black Magic" is far truer than it now appears. This is a deadly serious undertaking to those who choose to attempt to master this artform.

No cap in your rap. Keeping shit a G. A stack, one hundred…

To be committed to the craft and sincerity of the tongue is literally the way.

Rap had successfully influenced much of the known world and embedded itself completely as a pillar in the fabric of modern society.

Rap under the "Consortium of Rhythm" *an underground rap conglomerate/resistance* had undergone a rapid mutation. This allowed it to be actively used as a conduit to bring about what they believed to be positive change through teachings and content that promoted the understanding of oneself, spawning the creation of a self-sustaining free-thinking society. This event would force the hand of very powerful entities that seek to rid the world of melanated people.

No longer was money and vain pursuits of temporary pleasures to be the crux of rap/Black culture, just a symptom at best. This was the true orginal hue of the genre at it's conception. It's divine purpose.

If rap music was such a beautiful thing, why was it targeted by law enforcement?

Although the direction and intent to create a more purposeful and divine application of rap may have been the case for an under-publicized and intentionally suppressed sector of the worldwide rap industry, this was never the case when it came to what was primarily being focused on and promoted. A relatively small but meticulously organized group of influential right wing extremists who purposefully hijacked and engineered rap music and it's labels toward a grossly negative direction, aided in creating an infamous perception of our nature. These incredibly wealthy and powerful individuals met during the early 1990s and collectively constructed a system that engineered rap music to normalize death, homicide, and war into the culture which would bring about the death of our community and ultimately a seemingly self-inflicted genocide. It is not by mistake the mainstream media outlets disproportionately promoted rap and Black faces to the world in a negative light. Even the outlets that were not owned by these extremists would eventually be forced to play specific artists and records and none would face consequences for any bias. Many media platforms were secretly supported by investors of groups who backed their actions morally and financially. Together they conspired to create a new image of our people and capitalize off our ignorance which was the fuel to obtaining probable cause daily, leading to the over policing and mass incarceration discriminatorily of Black communities.

Any man who intimately studies sound and music understands the manipulation and weaponizing that occurred through the con-tent that was allowed into the multi-billion-dollar recording indus-try. The individuals responsible for the current state of our people understood the intricate science that exists within sound and the subconscious effects linked between a person's intention and the frequencies/vibrations that occur in music.

Certain frequencies tend to spawn specific moods and behaviors within the listener. These frequencies can also affect the listener's health and vitality. This information was kept hidden/dormant and intentionally set aside from common knowledge and curriculum throughout American history. This knowledge was instead used to weaponize vibration and groom our people with harmful intent. Powerful groups with the intention to do harm to our people would use these weapons against us. With a powerful medium such as rap music negatively aimed at our people, the dismantling of the Black race moved forward with unprecedented momentum. The plan was to push the industry in a direction that not only profited off the sale of confusion but actually caused it.

Although many people of all races and creeds were able to find salvation and refuge as rappers, eventually rap along with drugs and lack of civility would end up the purposeful blame for any unfortunate predicament of melanated people. The media moved forward to help the public digest this idea that Blacks needed saving from themselves and portrayed rap as the nucleus of our destruction when really, it was our light. The media focused on the negative narrative of rap which justified the war to eradicate it's true power, along with our people.

* William Chapman II * Eric Garner * William Howard Green * India Kager * Lawrence Hawkin * La'vonte Trevon Big * Oscar Grant * Victor Manuel Larosa * Eric Harris * Ryan Twyman * Calin Roquemore * Oladeinde Folahan * Michael Brown * Eric Harris * George Floyd * Amadou Diallo * Tanisha Anderson * Korryn Gaines * Breonna Taylor * Akai Gurley * Tamir Rice * Philando Castile * Rumain Brisbon * Jerame Reid * Matthew Ajibade * Frank Smart * Natasha McKenna * Tony Robinson * Anthony Hill * Mya Hall * Philip White* Walter Scott * Alexia Christian * Brendon Glenn * Victor Manuel Larosa * Jonathan Sanders * Nathaniel Harris Pickett Jr * Benni Lee Tignor * Miguel Espinal * Michael Noel * Kevin Mathews * Bettie Jones * Quintonio Legrier * Keith Childress Jr * Janet Wilson * Randy Nelson * Antronie Scott * Wendall Celestine * David Joseph * Dyzhawn Perkins * Christopher Davis * Marco Loud * Peter Gaines * Torrey Robinson * Darius Robinson * Kevin Hicks * Mary Truxillo * Tony McDade * Yvette Smith * Freddie Gray * John Crawford Ill * Dante Parker * Michelle Cusseaux * Arthur McAfee * Juan Pierres * Calvin Toney * Dewboy Lister * Anthony * Antonio Ford * Jamarion Robinson * Corey Tanner * Donnie Sanders * Dreasjon Reed * Josef Richardson * Antwun Shumpert * Isaiah Lewis * Marcus McVae * Gregory Griffin * Charles Roundtree * Daunte Wright * Aundre Hill * Manuel Ellis * Atatiana Jefferson * Aura Rosser * Stephon Clark * Botham Jean * Alton Sterling * Janisha Fonville * Gabriella Nevarez * Tanisha Anderson * Kevin Matthews * Sandra Bland * Khalil Ahmad Azad *

****

THE RAPTURE:

This event in history took place in the year 2058, when powerful and strategically placed decision makers of the government used several agencies including but not limited to the Military, police, FBI, CIA and Rap Enforcement Administration to wage war against rap music, ultimately becoming the tool White supremacists used to systematically eradicate melanated people.

Project Black Beam

1.

THE RAPTURE

The federal war on rap, *The Rapture*. The darkest days in American history since slavery and the civil war. Rapping became known federally as a component of many prominent groups considered by the government as terrorists. The federal government began citing rap lyrics that undermined the welfare of the nation to charge them in connection with actual events as well as videos similar to content created by terrorist organizations like ISIS and Al Qaeda. You know, jumping around waving guns in the camera, yeah that shit. They first began by garnering convictions based on lyrics of defendants, then ultimately lyrics would be used to outlaw the artform entirely.

Many remember it beginning with the outlawing of public gatherings and rap concerts. Quite naturally there was resistance from the public. Radio stations who refused to remove rap music from their airwaves received fines until they eventually were incapable of continuing business or were simply raided and immediately shut down. Laws required the music to be removed from store shelves and removed from public and personal media devices. Record companies were directed to seize and desist all current and future rap production.

Government agencies allowed rappers and producers to turn all rap associated media into authorities. They resorted to buybacks and even tax credits. Many people lunged at the opportunity but that method was ultimately too slow to achieve the far-rights objectives. Many people who heralded the genre rebelled. Soon after rebellions began to gain a stronghold law enforcement would commit themselves to storming and raiding personal and public property around the country around the clock. They then began to conduct full scale property raids of well-known rappers, producers, and engineers. Many of which were the leaders of movements to resist the oppressive regime. If you had beat making software on your computer, the government would confiscate it and you would be taken before a judge for sentencing. Your trap/gangster/rap style beats, authorities were taking them away.

Even down to your drum kits and synth samples. Police units were directed to storm homes across the United States to obliterate the institution of rap. Ripping posters off teenagers' walls and burning artist merchandise. Home by home people were marched into the streets and held at gunpoint while the government confiscated everything they could from every residence.

Prison sentences were given to people who refused to comply and were caught engaging in rap. You could get 5 years in prison if they found a Pierre Bourne snare or a Lex Luger sound in your sample library. Police were raiding people's vehicles finding tons of rap CDs and hard drives full of all sorts of rap associated media in trunks of cars. All of it was ordered to be confiscated as evidence in court and eventually destroyed. You could get arrested for wearing a baseball cap backwards or having your pants hanging off your ass. Gold teeth...outlawed. Big rims and tinted windows...outlawed. Even cornrows and locks for a brief period, outlawed. They would hose and gas anyone gathering at arenas and stadiums if rap music were to be played. Night clubs and house parties amicably shut down.

Some of us who love the craft and artform pressed forward in a guerrilla war against the system but were ill equipped for a fight against the military industrial complex and suffered disfigurement, dismemberment, punishment, and for far too many...death. Fatal police encounters with African Americans reached egregious levels with little to no judicial recourse.

The occurrence of assassinations of prominent rap moguls have been a part of covert operations long before the *"war against rap"* was publicized and fully legalized. Rappers who had begun to understand the advanced utility of rap music and free-styling were targeted and removed from the Earth through "contrived accidents" or under the guise of petty gang or rap beef. A few of the notable: Prodigy, Nipsey Hussle, Young Dolph, MF Doom, Tupac, Biggie, Lor Scoota, juice world, Daylyte, Mac Miller, B.O.B, LL Cool J, David Banner, Mick Jenkins, Cashflow Harlem, Nicki Minaj, IDK, Durk, Heavy D, Tierra Whack, Logic, Lotto, Andre 3000, MoneyBagg Yo, Lupe Fiasco, Killer Mike, Eminem, Meek Mill, Missy Elliot and countless other names that could continue farther than the duration of this text. After the Rapture, assassinations would be carried out openly under the protection of law.

Many other rappers would seek refuge and leadership positions among the Consortium of Rhythm headed by Locus the Great Father who after a decade of war were dwindled to very few numbers and could not sustain battle against the nation's military forces and militarized police state. They ultimately suffered defeat and were to be forever erased from history similar to the tragic massacre of Black wall street in Tulsa Oklahoma or like the "drowned towns"of the early 1900s.

The current state of the melanated race did not come about by mere happenstance or mistake. The events that continue to culminate and bring about our unfortunate disposition reared their ugly heads many centuries ago. These happenings and circumstances have been delicately scripted and carried out by design. Powerful entities whose true intent lay in darkness devised this outcome in service of their own agenda. Our ancestors allowed this to happen during a time that was relatively considered a utopia. The fight for the stability of our people appeared to be over to them and while they were distracted and content, they failed to realize subtle critical details about their predicament. They failed to notice the fact that far-right winged White supremacists were organizing and strategically being the face of authority in our very own communities. One could argue the civil servant was the modern slave catcher, the "overseer". Blacks fell into a recast culture that artfully excluded us from positions of power that held the responsibility of protection. This transferred critical power to outsiders who used these positions to re-enslave and ultimately eradicate us: The police, the judge, and the politician. To become a police officer was frowned upon and as a result men outside of these communities were left patrolling them. The culture actively punished those who worked alongside authorities which allowed weak and decitful men to commit seedy acts with no legitimate resistance from the neighborhoods they victimized. Historically, trends show that low-income communities are more likely to breed crime. The lack of resources in these concentrated areas was the driving force behind the illegal activity that residents desperately believed were timely solutions to situations that systematically placed them in uninhabitable environments.

***Broken Windows theory**- A criminological theory that states the visible signs of crime, anti-social behavior, and civil disorder create an urban environment that encourages further crime and disorder.*

Neighborhoods that are considered bad only tend to become worse because the opportunist wants to take advantage wherever they feel there is an avenue for them. Instead of being provided relief and opportunity these areas were provided more police, surveillance, and prison infrastructure. Children continued to be publicly steered away from becoming judges and politicians through images and campaigns ran on popular platforms and media outlets and more so encouraged to become drug dealers and entertainers through carefully vetted and crafted propaganda. While distribution of marijiuana became a fully legal enterprise, the melanated community was mostly excluded from taking advantage of this lucrative market by gatekeepers and the nearly unreachable startup costs which left very little chance of us becoming legitimate competition. Our community was quietly suffering from a lack of wealth and occupational contrast.

Designer drugs and scientifically engineered pathogens are consistently created by those who view us as their natural enemy and used as a means of eradicating our people. Mandated vaccines that contained formaldehyde and mercury disproportionately gave Black boys autism and VAIDS (*vaccine induced immunodeficiency syndrome*), while our lack of trusted Black biologists and doctors to combat these attacks on our people continue to leave us vulnerable.

Guidance and wisdom unifiedly absent from our people. The family structure was the first casualty of war. Identity and self-worth were also targets high on the enemy's *kill list*. Colorism has been playing a key part in distorting our identity and perceived worth. For example the plan went as follows: make the face of authority in their neighborhoods White, the God they pray to White, the garment of choice for your favorite protagonist White and the industry standard of beauty White. These idolized perceptions of things considered opposite themselves to this day serve as pillars of contradiction among our people. This is where parenting, mentoring, leadership, and an established sense of self-worth would have been vital to solidify. Those who look to destroy us knew they couldn't stop the global evolution of consciousness and elevation of our people that was coming without removing these values from our community. The place they all agreed to focus was the devaluing, dehumanizing, and eradication of the source of melanated people, The melanated woman.

2.

The melanated woman. Miss Universe. The living God. The Queen. The mother, grandma, auntie, sister, daughter. She, her, her, and her. The fertile ground for the seed. The root. The ever-rushing river replenishing and renewing the land. She is the keeper of the Divine Canal and the Holy Bosom. The Supreme Being. To this day she is still the only woman in the history of the planet to be kidnapped, placed In shackles and trafficked to foreign lands thousands of miles from her home across the Atlantic Ocean to be enslaved for over 240 uninterrupted years. Her homeland stripped of it's wealthy history and natural resources. Her men and children plucked from her reach for vile and monstrous means of profit. For hundreds of years her newfound enemy would force her and her female offspring to unnaturally adopt and successfully maintain the role of both man and woman. She remained steadfast in the face of an uncertain future in the belly of unyielding torment. A superhuman feat. Melanated people underwent centuries of subversive conditioning by iron-handed nations across the Earth who intended to avert a once proud and thriving race of people to be the opposite by embracing the will and tradition of greedy corrupt men. Men who expelled the needs of the melanated woman for their own carnal and archaic needs had appeared to become her only chance to avoid extinction. 240+ years of trans Atlantic human trafficking and oppression brought about undeniably hellish conditions for an overwhelming majority of the melanated race. It is estimated over 12 million Africans were forced into shackles and shipped across the treacherous Atlantic waters on boats in vile uninhabitable living conditions. The number does not include the melanated population of people indigenous to the americas who were also enslaved. This consequently became centuries of what appears to be irreversible trauma. The textbook definition of nothing short of the world's most devastated and disenfranchised race of people. Fiendishly victimized by the lustfully imperial ways of brutal and remorseless colonizers. It is said that no man could achieve total knowledge of God without complete oneness with the melanated woman and that no nation can rise higher than the status of it's woman. With her now under constant attack the world stage could be set for the destruction of our people. Colonizers across the globe had continued to unapologetically honor the traditions setforth by their ancestors with pride, love, and reverence. Meanwhile, the melanated people of the Earth were bound and constrained to a malicious and repulsive reality aggrandized to an inexplicable apex. This aided us in further losing our sense of self and true orientation with the universe.

Melanated people in the year of 1863 in the United States were granted freedom from slavery yet still received overwhelmingly harsh treatment and discrimination after freedom was granted. The 13th amendment outlawing chattel slavery as it was known would not officially be changed until 1865. Jim Crow practices, Black codes, and segregationist policies would be implemented nationally from 1865 through the 1960s. Which would by law make it disproportionately difficult for melanated people, especially the women to prosper. This included the right to rent or own land and access to proper banking. Renting and owning land was vital for the creation of a sustainable life and to build the generational wealth that their white peers acquired and benefited from. Many of these predatory laws were used to force melanated people into working for nothing or extremely low wages. Ex-Confederate soldiers working as police and judges made it difficult for Blacks to win court cases which enforced these predatory laws. Melanated people were threatened with as well as sent to prison for not adhering to these laws. Information outlets at the time were made to further the agenda to dehumanize and mock melanated people. Oftentimes melanated people were depicted as Blacks with big red lips and jet-black skin, dancing and prancing about. These depictions were created with the intent to illustrate us as being unbecoming and inherently incapable of having or obtaining substantial intelligence. They would also specifically depict our woman as an oversexualized harlot. These depictions were consistently proven false.

Shortly after the civil rights movement in the 1960s, broken homes and obsolete family structures consequently would be found more prevalent among melanated people. Blacks in the US are the offspring to victims who survived a massive global human trafficking ring. During chattel slavery, human breeding farms where one male was forced to impregnate multiple melanated women sometimes even his own family members by the hundreds with no intention of raising the children in a traditional family unit. Even after many years of our people incessantly fighting injustice, welfare systems provided by the government to aid underprivileged communities would perpetuate similar conditions through coerced separation of Black families with regulations that required a woman to be living alone or government assistance would be denied.

By the year 2019, 64,000 melanated women were reported missing in the US and mainstream media was directed to make little to no mention of it. This occurred during a time where for every dollar a White person made, Blacks in comparison only made 1 cent. Blacks were in a state of emergency, but this was the absolute norm. Widely popular fashion brands like Gucci and H&M were not owned by melanated people but were still revered by us despite their lack of sensitivity to the plight and struggle of melanated people across the globe, sometimes promoting advertising campaigns that resembled times in history when melanated people were considered less than human.

"No system oppressing you is going to allow you access to information that liberates you."

-Justin Blu

3.

FORT EVERS
WINTER 2108

"Let's just keep the arrangement the same, they got drones, foot patrols, and sensors everywhere. It's hot right now. Y'all been extra active lately. I aint tryna get screwed with two of us leaving the barracks," said Dubs.

"We got word straight from the top it has to happen now. He comes with you or no deal," replied the Dweller.

Dubs replied with a nod and clenched jaw. He heads back to the base from the lower wards just in time to walk into the barracks bay as the rest of the soldiers begin to head downstairs to formation. Dubs is a squad leader among the youth regiments within the U.S. Army and the 20th child to be successfully augmented with cybernetic attributes.

"X Listen, you're coming with me tomorrow," he says as he ties his locks into a ponytail.

His hands are decked with silver rings that match the silver in his arms.

"To the raids? Yeah, I know," X replied.

"No after the raids," Dubs says under his breath as he glances to his right as if to avoid others nearby.

X is the 10th child to be converted to a humanoid under Project Black Beam hence the 'X.' He knew Dubs supplied the soldiers with DMT (Dimethyltryptamine) and candy and would occasionally sneak out to the lower wards to get them. So, he understood exactly what he meant. DMT is the recreational drug of choice among a few of the soldiers since it didn't show up any different than the DMT your pineal glands pump through your blood already and a concentrated dose would wear off relatively quickly. The DFAC's *(dining facilities)* on base never feed the soldiers candy, so it's been considered a delicacy among the units. X is about 17 Years old going on 18 and Dubs is 18 years old going on 19.

X asks, "Whatever you need, but why me?"

"You got to go, talk to my guy, see what they want. They asked for you by name...I'll get you back home in one piece, you got my word," said Dubs.

As his battles *comrades run out the room to formation one after another, X thought to himself for a moment, "I would like to see a bit more of the wards close up...I need to see what's really out there...I always get good vibes about Dubs, he knows people outside of here and I need to figure out how."

X nods his head in agreement and jogs with the others through the doors to formation.

A soldier shouts, "Company, attention!"

In unison the entire company composed completely of young Black soldiers switch from a lax position to standing upright with their chins up and chests out.

"You have your orders, follow them," the commander crushes what's left of his cigar beneath the tip of his boot and continues pacing the front of the formation.

3 other high-ranking officers stand in front of 2 parked armored tanks overlooking 4 rows of 20 soldiers.

The commander, continuing to shout, yells, "I expect you boys to make nothing but uncut hell for your enemies out there tomorrow morning! OUSEYE?"*(Oouu-sigh*)*

"OUSUU!" *(Oouu-sue*)* The ranks bark in unison.

"You will crush them in their dwellings and in those holes they hide! OUSEYE?!"

"OUSUU!" the ranks roar again.

"Show them what it means to truly be elite. You represent order and honor. A brighter future…they represent confusion and chaos… darkness. They have chosen to live a life in rebellion of civility and for that their punishment will be death. Let no rebel combatant live to say a thing."

He says it with a placid demeanor.

The ranks stand like trees in the wind, heads facing forward, eyes peering into the distance.

A different officer begins to speak, "you will use every single fiber in your government issued behind to eliminate the threat and complete your mission! OUSEYE!"

"OUSUU!"

"Be proud as we bow our heads. Dear God, we are thankful to do your work. Watch over each and every one of these boys and instill in their hearts that a place in your kingdom is set for us and a place in hell has been set for each and every one of our enemies oh God,… Amen?" asks the commander.

"Amen!"

"Ouuseye?"

"Ousuu!"

It's early the next morning and a convoy of four armored vehicles leaving Fort Evers travel west through several of the lower wards. A small, unmanned aerial surveillance vehicle *drone** shadows them just beneath the clouds. As the convoy travels, X notices a few melanated people who the soldiers have grown accustomed to calling '*Dwellers*'. He sees them walking about the dusty sand filled roads and darting between the dwellings. They wear garments that resemble blankets and cloaks.

Aboard the convoy through a loudspeaker a voice is heard saying, "Lock and load, ETA 40 seconds."

X, alongside one of the soldiers, aboard one of the vehicles, rolls up his sleeve, and begins to run his fingers over his forearm feeling the metallic material and the blue lights that appear embedded in his skin. The convoy crosses under a highway in a run down abandoned looking section of the ward. Their target location is an old abandoned bar with worn painted lettering across the top floor spelling out *P's Pub*. The pub is attached to some garage units. Intelligence of Dwellers there engaging in class A ranked felonies has come to the attention of the armed forces nearby and this raid is the result. The rolling convoy immediately began taking fire from rebel forces. **Turturturturturt* A steady flow of rounds coming from the rooftop of the Pub causes the lead vehicles to swerve in a snake pattern to sidestep enemy fire.

A soldier shouts, "Rooftop 11 o'clock!"

A projectile fired from the UAV inbound just below the clouds strikes the top of the abandoned Pub. It explodes on impact and the firing seizes. The convoy surrounds the building, the soldiers hurry out their vehicle's rear and line themselves against them. A short dark-skinned man bursts through the rear alley door of the bar firing an automatic weapon in the direction of the soldiers who were taking cover behind the vehicles. Two other Dwellers run out from behind him and toward the opposite direction.

"Seize them!" One soldier yells.

"Contact 12 o'clock!"Another can be heard yelling from behind the armored vehicle.

Another soldier quickly extends his left arm in the direction of the short man as an electric charge shoots from that soldier's arm. The young soldier's arm blasts with a flash that blows the top half of the rifle-bearing man's body back through the door he barged out from.

"On me!" Sergeant Marshall yells as he lines up against the wall next to the door.

One of the teens taps Sergeant Marshall's shoulder signaling the others are in position to clear the building. They step over the remains of the man who initiated contact as they entered.

They enter through the door leading to the garage while violently kicking chairs, manikins, and other dusty items out of their way. A Dweller emerges from the group of manikins and grabs one of the teens. The teen picks the Dweller up by the collar and spears him through a concrete wall with a thundering crash. Other teens continue heading into a larger room with 2 ATV's, a basketball hoop, a recording booth, and a large painting of a nude dark-skinned woman on the wall above a couch. Half of the squad take the steps leading to another room while the other half continue forward. Another Dweller steps from behind the booth firing an assault rifle at the teens only for him to meet a barrage of returned fire from them.

"Target down, room clear," says a soldier in the unit.

They begin to smash the computer, rip chords, and foam paneling off the studio walls and set fire to the CDs and media they find in the room. The fire grew larger, lighting the dark room revealing the words *"Know Thyself"* graffitied on the wall. The soldiers continue to add any illegal media and technology found throughout the building. X takes a moment to read the word *"Mixtape"* written in black ink on a silver CD before tossing it into the fire.

"All this for one of these," he thought to himself.

"On me!" Sergeant Marshall yells from the other room.

5.

"You see the way I tossed that ol' hag when she came through the kitchen?" Asks 17 as he sat atop his bunk eating slices of an apple one by one.

He cuts himself another slice. Others join in with laughter. 17 is a tall slinky Black kid. He has a pointy nose and a bald head with the number 17 tattooed on the left side of his head. His tan undershirt is tucked into camouflage cargo pants that are tucked into his boots. He smells of sulfur and dry humor. Once he stuck his arm in a tank's gun to shoot off rounds into the chamber in an attempt to kill a Dweller who hijacked it.

"I don't give a shit, you know me. I'm not even waiting to see if they rap or harborin' it or some weapons or some shit.

I'm just shootin' niggas...," said 17.

"Outta here," says another with a grin.

"You can't let your guard down with them, they're all rebels down there. I swear to God I don't know why command acts like we don't know it," another teen adds.

X thought to himself in agreement.

"Ay X," said Dubs as he motions his head with a tilt, meaning let's go.

Command let the squad leaders have a bit more privileges and responsibilities around the barracks and around base. Dubs used this as the opportunity to leave undetected. Dubs had access to rooms X never saw. One of the rooms had access to the ventilation for the buildings. Dubs began to light candles he had in a duffle. Enough candles huddled together in a room resembled a body heat signature. This is how the military periodically kept track of how many soldiers were roughly present. The ventilation room had a vent they fit themselves into. The top of the vent directly touches the ceiling where Dubs had carved a makeshift exit through the inside of both the vent and roof which they used to leave.

"Keep your head down and move when I tell you," said Dubs.

The base uses drones and motion sensors to secure the grounds but Dubs was extremely perceptive and managed multiple escapes. He was great with patterns and strategy. None of the other teens in the bay could beat him in chess during recreation, he even beat the Sergeants, so learning when and how the drones behaved on routes and when to avoid the sensors was a task he could grasp overtime. The two narrowly avoid detection and brush shoelaces with death at several points during their exit.

RENDEZVOUS WITH THE DWELLER...

Dubs and X head into an old hotel lobby not too far from Fort Evers to meet the Dweller who asked for X. That same Dweller is also the one supplying the DMT. Sand and dust is settled across the floor and furnishings. The walls were trimmed with gold patterns against a black backdrop like something out of the roaring 20s. There were 2 armed Dwellers up on the mezzanine balcony staring down at X and Dubs as they entered.

A Black man and woman were each dressed in cloak-like items sporting metal binocular type goggles over their eyes. There was one sitting at the lobby desk, another sitting on the desk and one leaning up against it. They were Dwellers but didn't look poor like X was used to. The Dweller they came to meet name is Lennox *(Len- ox*)*. Lennox hopped down from atop the desk where he sat and walked toward Dubs and X. Lennox walked up to stand face to face with X, looked him up and down and said.

"This aint the kid."

Dubs and X shared a quick and confused glance.

"Are you afraid of death?" Lennox asked X.

"Huh?" X replied.

"Like are you ready to die for your unit?"

"I don't die for nobody."

The other Dwellers laughed.

"Nah this is X," Dubs says to Lennox.

Lennox does an about face and begins to walk in the opposite direction. As he walks away he says,"Yeah but that's not who we're looking for... they're raising a bunch of cowards over there. I wouldn't be down range too long with this one if I were you. Matter of fact, I'd put two in his head."

X scrunches his face in a mug. The Dwellers brace and move themselves into position to flank X and Dubs.

X thinks to himself, "I'll show him a coward...I wasnt tryna get into anything while we aren't even supposed to be out. We got no support down here."

"Cool it, X," Dubs whispers.

Lennox reaches into his pouch and tosses Dubs the batch of DMT he came for. "I promised you safe passage out, hang around too long and whatever happens is on you," says Lennox to Dubs as he returns to his seat atop the lobby desk and gestures his finger toward the exit.

THE NEXT MORNING

"Mission briefing in 5 minutes!" shouts a squad leader.

"The soldiers take their seats as the lights shut off and the briefing slides projected in 3 dimensions in the center of the room.

A high-ranking officer in the room begins to speak, "Colonel Pittman has green lit 8 combat operations against resistance forces for the next 72 hours with the intention to inflict severe damage and extract 3 high priority targets. 3 miles deep into the 9th ward a meeting with senior members of the resistance is scheduled to take place at 0800 hours. This is Intel confirmed by 3 sources. 5 tier 1 targets are expected to be present, Dominique Armoni Jones their top financial advisor along with Machete, formerly known as Gerald Green, Tyreek Trotter, Marcus J Hopsin, and Andre Benjamin III. These men are to be brought in alive as they will be critical assets for future operations. Because of the high value personnel being targeted, we will have senior level personnel doing the heavy lifting on this one. Sergeants Marshall, Cerney, Hayes, and Captain Burch will lead their units to engage and clear separate entrances of the building. Delta and Echo will be securing the perimeter and providing support for A and B. After arrival no one else in or out. The entire mission is to be no longer than 30 minutes in total. As usual the UAVs will cover you from the sky. The lower ward is extremely hostile. Expect resistance, do not underestimate them. Capture who we need, eliminate everyone we do not and bring everyone else home. OUSEYE!?"

"OUSUU!" the soldiers respond.

X laid in his bunk later that evening. One of the younger boys they called Smiley approached him.

"Some of the guys are saying this mission could be the one," said Smiley.

X sat up in bed.

"The one huh?"asked X.

"Yea, we catch these guys tomorrow and the war is over."

"Lights out, we gotta early morning tomorrow!" yelled a squad leader.

"Ay, this is it," said Smiley with his wide eyes focused on X as he walked backwards to his own bunk.

There was always chatter among the soldiers about the end of the war. X laid in his bunk through the night thinking about life outside the barracks. Life after the war. He always longed for the food restaurants served in the upper wards as opposed to the boiled eggs and rice the child soldiers were often served in the DFAC *(dining facility*)*. He dozed off but failed to sleep through the night. He'd been awakening from various dreams. In one of the dreams, X stood at an intersection in the desert. Buzzards pick at the remains of half a carcass. The road continued out of his field of view. In front of him a muscular shiny black horse is trotting nervously in a circle, stopping to stand on it's hind legs. Awake again in his bunk, he couldn't stop thinking about the Dwellers he met earlier and who the X they were actually looking for might be. He went over the mission briefing in his head and what his job was. He also pondered on if this was what he was meant to do with his life and was this all he was born for. He remembered hearing about what God's purpose for his children was and how his purpose was to serve the unit but tonight those words fell empty on his spirit. Melanated children were the only children serving in the Army. They were told after the war on rap was complete they'd be able to live normal lives like the other children born in the upper wards. He wondered if a life of hunting and killing the Dwellers was all he'd ever do. He didn't want to show it but he truly was worried about dying out there and the Dweller asking him about it was a bit surreal. He had seen many people including a few of the teens in his company die before and knew they would never come back. He didn't enjoy how no one really could tell him for certain what would happen in the afterlife. This made his stomach turn. He felt like his time was coming. X closed his eyes and shifted his body in his bunk to get more comfortable. Sometimes the metal in his arms would get cold and he'd sleep with his arms under his pillow.

Some of the soldiers began to get out of bed, shave, and get dressed. The bay lights turned on, X sat up with his feet dangling from the bunk to wipe his eyes. While leaving the barracks and heading to formation he stopped to pay close attention to a group of soldiers kneeling in front of a poster in a locker. Hanging was a depiction of Jesus with pale skin, a tunic, and sandals with one hand raised and the other hand covering his heart. X always saw them pray before missions. As he stood there, he imagined himself walking over and kneeling beside them to also pray.

SCAN FOR MORE CONTENT AND TO UNLOCK ADDITIONAL
CHAPTERS

8.

A soldier kicks in the side door of a red brick building and quickly steps back. 5 other fellow soldiers charge in single file through the doorway led by a soldier holding a riot shield. Each soldier crosses the threshold and goes in the opposite direction the previous.

"Military police get on the ground!"

They repeatedly yell as they search every corner of the room.

"Eyes sharp, they're in here!" one of the Sergeants yell.

"Split up, search everything, burn it down, top to bottom!"

X is outside of the building taking cover behind an armored truck. Locals watch from the street and various windows. X keeps a cautious eye. Spurts of gunfire ring out from inside the building for several minutes. A small canister is thrown from the doorway closest to X and explodes creating a dense white fog. Shots ring out and bullets begin to ricochet off the armored truck barely missing X. Some soldiers return fire through the smoke. X takes cover as he sees silhouettes running in the opposite direction of the building. One of them is Dominique Armoni Jones. X thinks to run after him but his feet couldn't quite move like he was used to, like they were frozen. His heart was pounding in his chest and ears and his hands had a slight shiver.

"Hey, stop!" yells X. Dominique stops running.

Someone yells, "Grenade!"

Everything flashes white.

X wakes up in bed, in a small dark black room he's unfamiliar with. There's a toilet, shower, sink, and black towels. Painted on the wall adjacent to where he laid was a black circle with a dot directly in the middle. He's badly injured but has been treated. Bandages are wrapped around his head. He is now wearing a black jumper. He slowly gets up and shuffles to the door to exit but it's tightly locked.

"Good evening, Alexander," a female droid's voice can be heard from a speaker on the ceiling.

X jumped, startled by the loud and sudden voice.

"Where am I?" X asked.

"A federal holding cell, you have been convicted of going AWOL and smuggling a schedule 1 substance onto federal grounds," the female droid voice says.

X eyes widened as he put both of his hands atop his head and took a deep breath. X thought to himself for a moment, so confused about what happened, he realized his unit commanders must have found out about him leaving somehow. Maybe Dubs told? Maybe one of the others. It was well known the penalty for being caught unlawfully outside the wire was the severing and replacement of control over your feet. The penalty for smuggling drugs into the base was death. They would gladly use your organs if you gave them a hint of espionage and blame your death on fratricide or failure to follow procedure. X still had his feet and his life but the thought of it pending was killing him inside. He sat back on the bed in disbelief with his hand over his face. His head was throbbing and the back of his neck itched. He ran his fingers across the back of his neck to feel a wound that had been stitched up. The tray slot in the door slid open and a pill with a cup of water was slid in before the slot quickly shut back. A full day would pass before X began to grow hungry. X was afraid of taking the pill because he feared death or waking up with his feet cut off. The slot slid open, a hand grabbed the tray and slid a new one inside with a pill and water before quickly shutting the slot back.

"What is this?" he yelled to the person on the outside of the door. The android interrupted, "a meal replacement pill containing the vital lipids, carbs, proteins, essential vitamins, and minerals the body needs."

X didn't trust the voice or the pill and sat without food or water for 2 days. He had never felt so weak. The humming from the vents seemed to make his head hurt worse than the injury.

He figured if he were to starve, he might as well take his chances fighting his way out. He stood as far back from the door as he could and got a sturdy stance and footing. He raised his right hand with his fingers toward the door and buried his face in the crook of his left elbow with just a hair of space for him to see. He charged the man cannon in his arm for 4 seconds.

"Warning, unauthorized use of firearms is prohibited," the android voice said as X blasted the doorway.

The blast appeared with a bright flash and hit the wall but collided with what looked like a blue hologram covering the room. The blast dented the wall slightly and dissipated through the hologram creating a wave throughout the room from where the blast struck. X lowered his left arm a bit to see his blast had done very little damage. Tired and desperate he had his mind made up to blast through the door, so he charged the man cannon in his arm again.

"Warning, unauthorized use of firearms will result in severe corrective action, warning."

X chuckled at the word firearm then shot a blast at the door again.

The hologram-like wall seemed to short circuit for a moment and returned a blast that slammed X into the back wall knocking him unconscious. X woke up with his head throbbing and a sharp pain in his lower back. With his stomach growling and aching and body in worse shape he crawled over to the tray, drank the water, and swallowed the pill. He laid his head down on the floor and stared at the wall.

After some time, X couldn't tell how long he had been in confinement. The program in the wall had said good morning about 30 times before she had gone silent. X laid still on the floor next to the slot waiting for the pill and the cup.

The slot slid open, and he grabbed at the person's hand shouting, "What're you waiting for!"

The hand jerked back before X was able to get a stern grasp on it. He could see them walk away wheeling a cart. He threw his pillow and mattress in the room in frustration and shoved his body against the wall in anger. When was he going to get out? He asked himself.

"What are you waiting on?" A voice asked from just outside the door.

"Who are you?"asked X.

No one replied.

X put his ear to the door and said, "I don't belong here."

"Where do you belong?"asked the voice from outside the cell.

"With my unit…they need me."

"Still loyal to the republic even as you await capital punishment I see."

X slid down to the floor with his back on the cell door.

"The republic..." X scoffed. "I care about my battles more than yall."

"What was your mission soldier?"

"Liberate the lower wards."

"Did it make you feel free?"

X thought to himself for a moment.

"No," he replied.

"So, what's the difference between being in here and being out there?"

X thought to himself again.

"I could at least make a difference."

Many days of only hearing his heartbeat or humming of the vent and occasional wheeling of a cart would pass. One day the slot of the door slid open and a piece of paper was slid into the room. The paper read *"Know Thyself."* He remembered seeing the same words on the walls during a few of the raids he conducted when he was on duty. He pondered on the meaning and was confused on who would slide the note under the door. Shortly afterwards, the android would begin to guide him through daily meditation and yoga. He also began to do pushups and other calisthenics as routinely as he could. He couldn't control being in the cell but he could control how he chose to spend his time. Pacing back and forth and assuring himself that one day he would be free provided him with some temporary relief. Day after day the pieces of paper with different positive messages, some he didn't understand, would be slid through the slot of the door.

Messages like:

Know Thyself
Life is happening for you not to you
Master your mind, master your build
Love yourself first every time
AMMO (AMbition MOtivation)
My life is abundant
I am blessed
I let go of everything that no longer serves me
I deserve to be happy
The point of life is to excel at the impossible
The universe always gives me everything I need
Joey's Story
I achieve my goals easily and quickly
Don't underestimate my intelligence
Abundance is my reality
I am perfect and everything I touch becomes special
I derserve the best
Elevate the world
To live is an awfully big adventure
Dont be afraid
No excuses

"There is no man alone, because every man is a microcosm and carries the whole world about him."
-Thomas Browne

13.

X awoke at some point to the door being open. He sat up questioning whether this was a mistake. He got up and walked out the door and proceeded down the hallway which led to a room with 2 black leather chairs adjacent to each other with a small table between them. There was a brown skinned man sitting with his legs crossed in one of the seats. He was dressed in all black wearing an embroidered cloak over a button up with 12 white stars down the sleeve.

"You gonna start talkin'?" X asked.

There was a moment of silence before the gentleman sitting in the chair said, "The kingdom of heaven is within you; and whosoever shall know himself shall find it."

X just stared at the back of this man's head in a silent confusion.

"Come have a seat," the man said as he laid his hand out in the direction of the seat in front of him.

X slowly made his way to the seat.

The man stood up, reached out his hand to X and said, "My name is Heka. I apologize that your stay here hasn't been pleasant but we are happy to have you."

X looked at Heka's hand and then to the rest of the room.

Heka sat back down and said, "Please, have a seat."

X sat and asked, "What is this?"

Heka replied with a chuckle," it's time for you to know..."

Heka looked at X for a moment and asked, "Have the nightmares stopped?"

X thought to himself and realized he had been getting more sleep than usual and couldn't remember having a nightmare since he was incarcerated. X looked around then raised his eyebrows with an aha moment type gesture.

"Good," said Heka with a smile as he continued, "the pills we offered you should be giving you a much-needed boost to the serotonin, norepinephrine, and dopamine transmitters in your brain. This is what's helping combat the conditioning causing the night tremors…you know, make ya feel good. You were told this is a federal holding facility. It is not."

X was clearly confused.

"And you haven't been convicted of anything… This is Amara. The first colony built underground during the Rapture.

We lied to you before because we needed you to accept this new reality in a way you would…accept. Once we confirmed eyes on you, we made plans to grab you."

"We? Grab me?" asked X with a muddled tone.

Heka rubbed his chin with his pointer finger for a moment as the two shared a locked gaze.

"We are who you would refer to as the 'Dwellers, the resistance… the undesirables."

"What?"

"But we refer to ourselves as the CORR."

(Core* - *The Consortium of Rhythm and Rights)*. Also known as the Consortium of Rap.

"We've been living deep in the ground away from the war and the raids."

X looked horrified with his mouth agape as Heka continued to explain.

"We've recovered other children like you in the past and sometimes to no avail. We outright told them the truth, but their conditioning was too ingrained for us to free them. So, I designed the cell in which you've been living. You sleep to binaural beats and the supplements you've been taking are to ease the process."

"Free Them? Process? What do you want?"

"Yes, to show you the truth and allow you to make your own decision after that, it's quite simple actually."

"What Truth? Talk fast!" X demanded as he balled up his fist.

"The truth about you. The truth about us. They took you as a child far before you could remember and chose to turn you into one of these," Heka pulls a pistol from his hip and places it on the table then Points to X's arm.

Heka stood from his seat as a projection appeared next to them showing black and white images of Louis Farrakhan, Dr Martin Luther King, Sojourner Truth, Marcus Garvey, Malcolm X, Shirley Chisolm, Fred Hampton, Rizza Islam, Dr. Umar Johnson, and Angela Davis. The slides and film continued, some in color.

"Your leaders. They suppressed and murdered many of your real leaders. Our leaders. We've been at war with them in this country hundreds of years before you were born, and in conflicts with them thousands of years before that. They've hidden this from you. Made you a weapon against your own people."

X looked away confused then began to reply,

"I've seen the videos myself, Dwellers killed each other every day. Dwellers made the music that controlled the minds and polluted the Earth. Rebels, terrorists. Yall destroy yourselves and anyone who gets in your way."

"That is the lie you've been told. It did not always appear this way. The same people telling you to destroy us and rap music are the same people who made sure rap music and our appearance had that effect."

"How? They wouldn't do that. They saved me, rap is what destroyed my people and my home. It's a plague on us. It's the reason why I don't have a family and why the lower wards are in ruins, don't you see with your own eyes?"

"I will do my best to show you the truth but you must remain willing to question the things you already know...Locus the great father led the resistance in war many years ago against your captors in a time where rap was freely used throughout the planet. He and the other originals understood the truest application of rap. They were able to create a lifestyle and simple methods for anyone willing to walk the path to master it. A path focusing on self-knowledge, balance, and dichotomy in all things. They employed empathy, astrology, anatomy, the inalienable Godly nature that exist within all things. Chakra, a mastery of language, diet and the constant pursuit of a life walked in a self-correcting path. Not just the destructive forms of sound you were taught destroyed our people. He and his most dedicated and loyal students taught that through true improvisation through freestyle rap one will simultaneously create flows and vibrations that have an incredible and immediate impact on one-self and the surrounding environment. Through this he was able to amass incredible amounts of loyal students. His goal was to create a subculture within rap which highlighted the spiritual nature of the genre. To progress rap into an evolved form of a respected religion so to speak. One oriented in creating a reality without meaningless suffering, unnecessary ailments, and to promote an abundant mind-set. The value of an abundant thinking society without unhealthy attachment to money or vain pursuits becomes priceless. Love, em-pathy, and understanding of oneself in accordance with nature they believed would bring about the manifestion of heaven on Earth," said Heka.

"If what you say is true, what happened to them then? Did they become corrupt or something?"

"No they did not change but this did not please those commonly referred to as 'the powers that be', the Folks who made you the way you are. The ones who order you to kill us. The ones we've been fighting for hundreds of years. They preyed on the weakness of the masses. They exploited our lack of self-love and self-control and our obsession with vain pursuits of controlling the material realm. Rap under the Consortium of Rap is being used as a conduit to bring about change, understanding of oneself, and promote the self-sus-taining free-thinking society. All the good work we do undermines the control of the most powerful entities in the world. No longer is money and vain pursuits of temporary pleasures to be the crux of rap and Black culture. This was the true original hue of it's concep-tion, it's divine purpose. Rap only primarily became the overtly de-structive and perverted version of itself by the meddling of cultural outsiders and capitalistic agendas. Powerful and wealthy individuals who have no vested interest in the welfare of the people that become byproducts of the tainted culture. They have no interest in spiritual matters and have been taught for centuries to destroy melanted people and those who love them. Lockhart Williams, the people responsible for enslaving you partnered with private entities who were rooted in Neo-Nazi leadership and ideals with vested interests to infiltrate the culture of rap. They became the gatekeepers of how it would be spread and to promote our own demise. Rap has become a worldwide phenomenon regardless of their efforts to contain it to just our communities. They couldn't outright stop the spread of rap, but they knew because of our weakened collective state they could manipulate the flow of content that could enter the global multi-billion-dollar industry that was loved across the world. Privately owned weapon companies like Lockhart Williams have throughout history made it their business to spread darkness and amass power at the expense of the Nations without consequence. As American society walked into a state of comfort and leisure these same steps led us to exist as puppets of naiveté. It was as if it didn't hit home, it didn't happen. For many of our ancestors the powerful and cohesive information didn't hit the next generation. If just one of them could have rallied our people before things got out of hand or just one person could go back and warn our people about what was happening, maybe we could have avoided what should be known as the slaughter of billions of innocent people. These groups who are now almost completely in control today have hated us for longer than we know. They targeted the reward centers in our brains. It was a new drug that no one knew how to detect. The most powerful drug of them all. Children like you walked around with computers in their pockets that spewed the music you've been taught we seemed to enjoy the most, while outsiders to our communities reaped the wealth that stemmed from the electronic ignorance of our people. Before they knew it, it was too late. By the year 2022, Blacks only accounted for about 12.5% of the US population and this number continued to dwindle. This was induced through the weaponizing of music and of our skin," said Heka as he used his hands to command the digital projection.

"Here, one of our founding fathers who your captors fought tirelessly to destroy, listen to his words closely."

A projection of Locus the Great father stood and began to pace the room and speak.

"They always feared the prophecies would come true and end their reign of confusion and man's disconnection with our creator. Music is a gift given to man. Music is the way to unlock and eradicate subconscious blocks and aid mankind in escaping the great void. This knowledge has been forced into the shadows of society for millennia because those who seek to liberate the masses also seek to undermine the elite. Rap, regardless of any current opposing use and conception, is innately a divine activity. One who studies and becomes immersed in this artform will inevitably arrive at the conception of oneself at a universally divine level. One who lives life in relentless pursuit of truth and genuine expression will find the truest form of self. This is what is and has always been feared by the elite who have always known this truth. The greatest rappers to ever do it only scratched the surface of the boundlessness that exists and remains dormant and untapped. Those who know the truth understand that rap music as we experience it currently is in it's infancy. We have barely begun to see what rap really is and despite our highest praises and devices are only flattering the unfathomable beauty of it's full expenditure. Members of the 'Consortium' refer to this state of being as the 'God Tongue'. This is the ability to accurately articulate one's true dispostion through utilizing improvisation employing rhyme schemes and seamless flow accompanied by pure intention of the heart and connection with the source of all creation which we commonly refer to as God. This is a very powerful state of being we have yet to experience. Power that could obliterate the greatest armies. The flowing, deciphering, decoding of reality and creation in real-time is the act in which tunes us directly into the vibrations and frequencies of our creator, who is the energy existing within all creation. This is the highest act any soul can perform. Rap is prayer evolved. This is the moment when words create vibrations that ripple unbounded through space and time to bring about the existence of heaven on Earth. Throughout time this truth has been hidden from the masses by elites who conspire against this divine shift. This truth is hidden by those who contribute to the unholy theft of rap's original God given purpose. Which is for society as a collective to work towards attaining and harnessing this Sublime state of being. They have through genocidal and barbaric means successfully thwarted and replaced what should have been coveted by the heart of the world as it's collective goal with what is relatively minuscule, petty and in every sense of the word blasphemous pursuit of mansions and record deals. The material world is beautiful, Godly and serves it's divine purpose when orientated in accordance with natural law. However, when in direct opposition to natural law it serves to confuse and aid the world in a subconscious exchange of the impenetrable and unfathomable beauty of heaven on Earth for lifeless and ever crumbling brick and mortar. Until rap is untainted and culturally revered for the spiritual act that it is, the world will be left to it's ever-failing devices and vain treasures of the lost who know nothing of their true being."

The projected transmission ended. Heka sat on the edge of his chair and continued.

"For very short times throughout history melanated people began to channel and honor the spirituality and sciences of their ancestors. This information supported the spiritual nature behind sound and the subconscious link between intent and the effect the frequencies and vibrations would have on the behavior and health of the listener. These are the very uses of sound that healed the body and erected temples that still baffle the greatest doctors and engineers of today. These are considered the Golden Ages of music and several Golden

Ages exist. One of the more recent from 1970-1987 contained disco or soul music which targeted and healed the soul, our chakra system by promoting love and unity with the timbre of live instrumentation and or deploying vibrations emanating from recordings on vinyl records. The vibrations allowed people across the Earth to remember who they were and the spiritual agreements they made before journeying into the physical plane. This spawned a mass awakening.

Chaka Khan with *"Do you like what you feel"*
Tina Marie with *"I Need Your Loving"*
The System with *"Don't disturb this groove"*
Loose Ends with *"You can't stop the rain"*
Mary Jane Girls with *"All night long"*
Heatwave with *"Send out for sunshine"*
Earth, Wind & Fire with *"Let's Groove"*

These are songs that brought listeners closer to their divinity and in tune with our creator.

Alicia Myers *"I want to thank you"*
Cheryl Lynn *"Got to be real"*

And countless others. I urge you to join us, if you truly want to make a difference in this world as you say. Join us as we celebrate, create, spread, and protect masterpieces like our ancestors who channeled divine messages designed to heal you and connect you with the source. Notable Producers like Quincy Jones and Berry Gordy tapped into their DNA and mentality and began to decipher reality to achieve higher states of consciousness. They were spreading waves through mainstream media bringing unity and heaven on Earth! We gotta do the same if we wanna raise the people and bring about the future we deserve."

X sat and watched the projections of people dancing and singing together. Images he was never shown. Songs that made the hair on his neck and arms stand. He listened as every word fell into it's own place in his heart. He knew his life would never be the same once he woke up in that cell and that this could actually be the opportunity to make a real difference. X looked at Heka speechless. A young brown skin, almond shaped eyed woman with her hair in a bush accompanied by a levitating chrome ball the size of a cantaloupe walks into the room.

"It's time," she says.

X recognized her voice.

"X, can I show you something?" asks Heka as he stands up to leave. X nods, stands up as well, then follows Heka out the room.

SCAN FOR MORE CONTENT AND TO UNLOCK ADDITIONAL
CHAPTERS

21.

X, Heka, and the young woman with the levitating chrome ball *(Sanctorium*)* walk into a small room with a rectangular window peering into a much larger room. The larger room is a dome with 5 rows of dirt mounds the length of the larger room. Through the window X sees a man walking from behind. The man stops, positions himself in a horse stance. He then takes several deep breaths.

The man then begins to slowly move his hands as if he were fighting. Fighting without worry and aggression. Finally with both hands stretched out in front of him he begins to recite a chant. His hands once again begin to move.

> *"Life, in abundance we speak*
> *Blessed is this land of the meek*
> *To harvest for generations to eat*
> *With open hearts and open minds*
> *Please offer your life as I offer mine"*

He repeats the simple rhyme as he continues to slowly move his arms. The ground begins to rumble. The hairs on X's arm stand. The chant continues.

"With open hearts and open minds
Please, offer your life as I offer mine"

The man continues to chant as the ground trembles. Green stems slowly emerge from every row of the dirt mounds. For about 5 minutes it lasted. X couldn't believe what he was witnessing. He was taught that plants would take weeks to grow at this rate.

"How is this?" X nervously asks.

"It is the power of rap," the young woman responds.

"This is how we feed our people," said Heka, "this is what they never intended for you to know."

X continued to feel chills from the top of his head down the back of his spine. Everyone walks out into the larger room. X bends down to observe the stems protruding from the ground. He fondles one.

He gathers himself and asks, "did he really offer his life?"

"Yes." Heka responds, "When his time on Earth is done, his soul will reach nirvana and his body will return to the ground from which it originated to be the nutrients for mother Earth just as she has been for him. So will we. I know this is all new to you but even still I must take this time to ask you. Will you allow us to build you in the way of the Great Father? We believe you could be a great asset to free this world… If you decline, we will take you away from here where you will be free to go as you please."

X nervously looks away as he unsurely utters, "I…"

The young woman intercedes and says, "He is hungry, let us enjoy a meal and he will then have the answers he searches for."

"Heather is correct," replied Heka, "we shall eat."

SCAN FOR MORE CONTENT AND TO UNLOCK ADDITIONAL
CHAPTERS

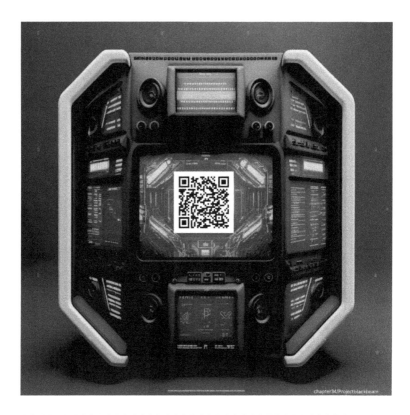

****

"No, I'll go."

Later that evening X sat alone in his cell, with the door now unlocked he sat inside pondering on what his life was to become. Heather knocks lightly on the open door, "Are you alright?"

X doesn't reply.

"I can see the heaviness weighing on your mind, I'll leave you to it but if you want to talk, I'll be just down the hall." She turns to walk away.

"Wait," says X.

Heather turns to face X.

"Why me?"

Heather walks further into the room and sits on the recessed wall that acted as a counter or shelf and begins to speak, "for nearly a century the CORR has studied the ancient metaphysical science of the relationships numbers and letters have with personalities and events throughout our lifetime. One of our elders, La Sirene, told us great leaders would be born among the batches of melanated transhumans. Ones that would help lead our people to heaven on Earth. She also knew which life path numbers you'd have."

"Life path numbers?"

"Yea. Our techies can sometimes hack the military's database where we can acquire intel. After a few hours of work, we knew exactly who we wanted to grab first."

Her floating chrome ball Sanctorium projected notes.

"See:

Alexander Mondane:

Your birthday is February 7, 2092.

That's	*2+7+2+0+9+2*
Which was basically	*9+13*
Which adds up to	*22*

You were the only one in your class that has that life path number. We couldn't let it go to waste."

"22?"

"Yes. This is the most powerful life path number of them all. It's up to you to use it to manifest what you desire."

X looked at the projection with glowing eyes. He felt a sense of calm come over him after the realization of who he was after all these years. He looked further into the notes to see his full name, he was never told his full name.

Alexander Mondane

135515452-4754155

135615459-4654155

Destiny Number 6. Soul urge number 2. Dream number 4.

The profile has all types of information about who he is.

"Someone will harness the 'God Tongue' of the prophecies soon. It's an exciting time," Heather said with a smile.

"I would like to be built in the ways of the Locus the great father," X replied.

Joy came over Heather for a moment as she looked at X.

"Locus The Great Father," she corrected him with a chuckle. "Alright, I'll let the others know…It's a brave thing you're doing. You didn't ask to be born into this world or to be made into a weapon for them but still you find the courage to go against them. I think La Sirene was right about you," she said before leaving the room.

"The world will ask you who you are and if you don't know, the world will tell you."
-Carl G. Jung 1875-1961

CHAPTER 55

Heka stands in the doorway of X's cell as X lies awake in bed.

"Good morning," says Heka, "Heather tells us you're ready to learn the way."

X gets up and stands facing Heka.

"Good morning, I am."

"Good, then let's be on our way."

X follows Heka through several corridors of the complex. They pass through a 10 story high living quarters where Dwellers and other members of the CORR live. The Phyllis Wheatley suites they call them. Way up in the ceiling there's a dome painted with a horse drawn chariot in the clouds of a blue sky. A bell is heard being struck in the distance. Everyone is clapping and smiling as they face the pair. Heka continues walking as if nothing is happening. X notices the bloody wrapping around Heka's right hand. People are bowing and tossing daffodil petals in the air as the two pass. X catches up to Heka and asks him what is going on.

Heka responds, "They are celebrating you and what you are about to do."

X lowers his head in response to those who bow to him. The pair at last arrive at the train station underneath the complex.

"We're headed to one of our sister colonies further north for your process. We've noticed a pattern of skirmishes in this area. It'll be safer to do things further north until you're done," says Heka.

The train arrives with a screeching halt. A short, round, brown, bearded fellow wearing a vest, goggles, and gloves with the fingers out steps from the train's conductor compartment. His clothes lightly brushed with spots of oil and grease. He greets Heka with a smile.

"Good to see you again brother," says the bearded man to Heka as he puts his hand on Heka's shoulder.

"Good to see you as well brother," says Heka with a smile.

"This is him?" the bearded man says as he motions his head toward X.

"Yup."

"Welcome to the Underground railroad mate." The bearded man says. "It's a bit of ways out but I'll get ya there in a jiffy, we've got but an iota of time to spare."

They board the train. Inside there's a lot of chatter among the passengers. X takes a seat near several other passengers. Heka stands at the doors holding the rail. The train is dusty and worn down. The lights sometimes in the cars often flicker, and graffiti is everywhere. About 30 minutes into the train ride, Heka takes a seat next to X. He closes his eyes as the train zips through the tunnel.

"The conductor your brother?" asked X.

"We're all brothers," Heka replied with his eyes still shut.

Not too far from where they sat a conversation was had between a pair of twin teenage Black boys.

"Yo Quay *(Kw-A*)*, look at this."

The twin points at the old ad in the ceiling while laughing. The other twin looks. It's a photo of a cracked egg in a frying pan subtitled, *'This is your brain on drugs'* with a government hotline to call to get rehabilitated and or report drug dealers.

The other twin laughs and says, "More like this is your brain if you trust the government."

Another passenger chimes in, "They want you call a number knowing they the ones was smugglin' the shit."

A few of the passengers laugh. One twin gets up to look at other ads when he notices X's arms.

"Ay, you one of them trans-humanoids ain't you?"

X looks at Heka whose eyes remain shut for a response and then back to the teen.

"Yea," X replied.

Chatter and gasps among the passengers briefly fill the car.

"What you doing down here? You must be in some shit you down here," says the twin.

Other teens gather around to take a look.

"I aint seen one up this close before ," one of the teens says.

"Do it hurt?" ask another.

The other twin reaches out his hand.

"I know you good people, you with him," he points to a sleeping Heka.

"I'm Jamyro (*Ja-my-row**) and my brother's name is Quay," he adds as they shake hands with X.

"I'm X and this is Heka, he's been sleep half the ride."

"I'm here," Heka replied, eyes still shut.

"Don't mind me just dwelling in the house of the most high."

"You're what in what?" says X.

"Next stop, New Karnak," the Bearded man says over the train's intercom.

The train enters a brightly lit station and comes to a halt. New Karnak is located under an abandoned impoverished city on the west coast in the lower wards.

The bearded conductor steps out of the driver's compartment, "Y'all ain't in here getting gobby are ya?" he says while laughing.

As the other passengers exit the train Heka opens his eyes and stands up. He puts his hand on the conductor's shoulder and nods with a smile then leaves. X follows as they make their way through the station.

"Those teenagers, they from the upper wards?" asks X.

"No," Heka responds.

"They aren't augmented like me though."

Not every newborn was turned over to your captors for augmentation. They are the children we could hide below the cities," said Heka.

The sister colony's train station was spotless, made of mostly glass with a huge tree planted in the center of the lobby surrounded by a library, school, repair shops, and places to buy and trade goods. "Tribe" by Jidenna plays from a sound system at a nearby fruit stand. Fruits are arranged and sorted in every color. Heka grabs two red apples and tosses X one. Vendors and patrons of all kinds were gathered shoulder to shoulder, some selling African masks and figurines all the way from Ghana and Benin. Beautiful women of every age and shade are trying on waist beads, sniffing oils and engaged in commerce. People with leopards and monkeys as loyal companions squeezed through the narrow openings in the crowd. Engineers are tinkering with bots and brandishing an array of different devices. Balloons and bright fabrics hang from walls and displays seemed to eclipse the sounds from the crowd with their loud and vibrant colors. Beautiful purses, bags, and paintings of melanated people with strong dispositions and unapologetically Africanoid features to be admired are in every direction. Children run freely between the crowds of merchants and patrons. X is rightfully taken aback by it all. As the population of Blacks began to grow in the underground colonies over the previous years, they had eventually formed monarchies to govern the underground territories as Kingdoms. Many other races of people live in the lower wards and in the colonies but the overwhelming majority of the population are Black. About 3,000 Blacks live in the underground colonies. A small population of around 5,000 Blacks live above ground in various parts of the world. The ones that live in the lower wards are known in the upper wards as 'Dwellers' and are tracked and monitored with microchips that go beneath the skin. The ones who know of the colonies that operate and exist in secret oftentimes gave their lives to keep these secrets. These people usually lived in abandoned structures and makeshift shelters they built themselves.

The lower wards are dilapidated and left to ruin and can span across over 30 miles at a time. 600 people may occupy this 30 mile radius in various living arrangements. These people are subject at any time to brutality by authorities, human trafficking, and other violent crimes by outsiders. On the contrary, the wealthy engineers and investors who built the upper wards saw it fit to build vertically. These wards are densely built and highly secure. They are closely governed and monitored by authorities that operate on systems that perpetuate the extinction of melanated people. The underground colonies were the only place Melanated people could seek refuge from the republic's traps and systemic schemes. Operating underground is their best chance at supporting rebel efforts within the CORR.

Heka and X continued to make their way through a sea of mela-natenated people within the temple and towards a stairway in the distance. A gentleman wearing a black thobe with 12 white stars on the sleeve waited at the bottom of the steps. He spoke.

"Greetings gentlemen."

"Greetings Abdul," Heka responds.

Abdul motioned for X to raise his arms. X raises his arms as Abdul pats him down. When X lowered his hands Abdul noticed the weaponry in his arms and looked at Heka with concern. Heka responded with a gentle nod signaling that it was ok. Abdul led the pair upstairs into a waiting area where a small group of people wait-ed outside tall double doors.

"Heka!" One of the people from the group shouted as the group hurried to greet him.

"Introduce yourselves," says Heka.

"I'm Destiny," says a boyish young brown skinned woman with her hair in braided locks.

"I'm Bradley," said a short muscular dark skinned young man,"but you can call me Brodie."

"I'm Rodney, I'm from the 9th ward," says another.

"I'm Gerald," said a chiseled faced gentleman with broad shoul-ders.

"I'm Alexander, people call me X."

"And I'm Jay Byrd," said another gentleman who cast a shadow over the rest when he stood.

Heka looked at his watch and then made his way to the door. He knocked 6 times.

"Who is it?" said a voice from within.

"It is I, Heka and with me I bring 6 others ready and willing to dedicate their lives to the CORR."

"You may enter," the voice responded from within.

They walked through the doors and between 2 pillars into a large dimly lit atrium with 4 men and a woman who sat shoulder to shoulder on one side of a rectangle shaped table that faces the door. A squad of armed melanated warriors stand guard behind them. The group entered and stood before the table.

"This the best you have to bring the CORR Heka?" says one of the gentlemen at the table.

"What is this rubbish you brought before us?" says another.

"They are unworthy, remove them at once," says another.

"Let's go," Heka says to the group standing before the council.

A bewildered look fell on the faces of the group of teens.

Heka leads them to the lobby.

"Wait here," says Heka.

He re-enters the room and shuts the doors behind him. Shouting and deliberation can be heard from the outside of the thick doors.

"Really?" says X.

"They sound like they wanna fight," said Destiny, "we can fight. I don't care."

"Right," said Jay Byrd.

Gerald shakes his head.

Bradley puts his head close to the doors to listen.

"We good just wait right here like he told us," says Bradley.

The doors open once again. Heka shuts the doors behind him as he exits. He turns around and knocks at the door again 6 times.

"Who is it?" the voice is heard from within.

"It is I Heka and with me I have 6 others ready and willing to dedicate their lives to the CORR."

"You may enter," the voice responds.

The group once again enters and stands before the council who now have a 7 branched candelabrum lit at the center of the table.

"I guess they do look a bit squared away," says a member of the council.

"Yeah, they're alright," says another.

Heka looks at the group of teens he entered with and speaks to them.

"We will serve as your commanding officers, drill instructors, and guides for the duration of your training but within the temple walls we will be known to you as your Prophytes. We will be guiding you in the ways of the consortium and through the curriculum of the Great and Honorable Father. You will look to and listen to us as you would your own parents. If you wish to succeed you must allow for our teachings to penetrate your hearts. Only then will the transformation take place."

One of the council members begins to speak.

"I'm T-Bone, known to disseminate rhythms of life and vibrations of love throughout the lower wards. I'm excited I can't lie. You will reactivate this chapter and bring much beauty to the wards."

T-Bone was a short, balled, brownskin, heavyset man, with a bearded face and a distinctly protruding belly.

"Next to me is The Mac, a father of a newborn and our armorer *(gunsmith*)*."

The Mac was tall and fit and wore a black thobe with pinned medals and honors.

"Next to him is OG3 the lead instructor here for combatives and your dean."

OG3 is a young umber skinned man also sporting a thobe, a well groomed militant fighter.

"Next to him, the lovely princess Ciara Leone, the daughter of our most noble King Anthony and Queen Tianna. She is the head of our history program here."

Princess Leone fashioned a crown and pearls which rested on her obsidian skin.

"On the end is Machete, a modern day Toussaint L'Overture. He led our warriors to countless victories including those over the U.S. Marines during Operation Compton Liberation and the battle of the bay."

Machete is tall, dark and sturdy, dressed as if prepared to raid a building with his vest strapped and his boots laced. Built like an olympian.

"Line up according to your height, shortest first," said T-Bone.

They shuffle about.

"Hurry Up!" yells Machete.

T-Bone once again begins to speak, "I'm interested, tell us why you here."

The group of teens don't say anything.

"Not all at once," he laughs with a big smile.

"You first," he said as he pointed to Bradley, the shortest one.

"I always liked the way the CORR carried themselves. A lot of my friends joined the CORR." He nervously looks at OG3. "And I want to fight for my people."

"You," says T-Bone as he points to X.

"I want to study the way, learn the truth and fight for what's right," says X.

"We understand you come from the child camps under *Project Black Beam*, correct?" asks Princess Ciara Leone.

"Yes, Ma'am," says X.

Rodney the 3rd tallest speaks.

"This is something I always wanted to do as a kid. I finally got my chance, I'm here to work."

T-Bone says, "This has been a long time coming for you, I'm proud of you."

Destiny speaks, she is the 4th tallest.

"I seen the fellowship work, and I'm tryna send a few of these rednecks back to hell."

Gerald speaks, "I seen how the CORR changed things and stood up for us growing up and I always wanted to do the same."

Jay Byrd the tallest of the bunch began to speak,

"Growing up I felt like I was the one to look after my family. I always wanted a brotherhood and to be there so the next person wouldn't grow up feeling like I did."

"You've been studying to become a biochemist, correct?" asked T-Bone.

"Yes," said Jay Byrd.

"I'm sure y'all are aware but this might be your first time hearing this so listen up. If the federal agencies discover us and or your involvement with us, you will be convicted of treason and sentenced to death. Just making sure that's clear. We are at war but at the same time in the service of others and as officers you will be responsible for commanding lives besides your own. What you are about to undergo is a grueling process that not everybody gets the privilege to partake in. You are here to not only become members of the CORR but also serve as officers of the Gamma Omicron Rho (**ΓOP**) division under the psi chapter."

The one known as The Mac begins to speak.

"Gamma Omicron Rho has been a secret division of the CORR for over 50 years. It will be up to you to prove your worthiness and to maintain the prestige associated within the organization. We are here to protect and rebuild our way of life."

Gamma Omicron Rho is a division of the CORR based on Greek interpretation of the teachings and traditions of ancient mystery schools that originated in ancient Egypt.

OG3 begins to speak, "Y'all work directly under my chain of command, you do what I say, any hang ups I'm hanging yall up."

"Period," Ciara Leone adds.

The one known as Machete speaks.

"This ain't a game. You listen up and shut up and you might get through. The council has chosen you to be trained in becoming effective leaders among the CORR. Show us what you've got."

The rest of the day was completely focused on developing a daily routine to handle training during the day and becoming officers of Gamma Omicron Rho at night. OG3 showed them to their living quarters and shared tons of insight and information on things like the organization's history and how to survive the process as he and his line did many years before them.

"These are y'all notebooks, everything we tell you, write down in your notebooks and study together each night. Everything in yall notebooks should be exactly the same. Every letter, every space. Every scratch, every dot. If not, we ripping them up or worse."

X could tell he was serious.

"Y'all might not understand what's going on right now but just know everything happening for a reason. I'm not goin' let nothing be done to y'all that wasn't done to me. Listen to what I tell you and you goin make it. Every day is a new challenge and it get harder and harder but it's only as hard as yall make it. No sex, no chatting, and talking in public places, no eating in public places, no elevators, escalators, or gliders. No black, silver, red, brown, or white foods. If you drop or get dropped from Omicron Rho, you also get denied entry into the CORR and will be forced to recycle into next year's class. You only get one shot to get into Omicron Rho though, so yeah don't give up. When one of us ask you, Babt? You say Babt back. That means building a better today but back in the day it originally meant building a Blacker tomorrow."

The group took copious notes.

"Don't write that last part, some stuff only gets written in yaw heads. Tonight, is simple, 2am we meet in the underground railroad. When we say 2 that means 1:50 for yall, don't be late," says OG3.

"Wake Up!"
-Dap, School Daze

89.

It's 2am. Machete, OG3, and The Mac stood in front of their 6 Neophytes who stood in height order on the platform of the train station. The Mac wearing sunglasses, a green beret, and a black jean jacket with black fur on the collar walks to the first neophyte Bradley.

"Lead your line to go stand on the tracks," The Mac says.

Bradley looks to OG3 confused. OG3 nods his head toward the direction of the tracks giving him the ok.

Bradley says, "Let's move," and heads toward the tracks.

The others follow. The Mac walks to the edge of the platform and kneels. He pulls out a vape with the temperature reading on the side.

"Come here," he says to Bradley, "open up."

"Pause," jokes Machete. Bradley opens his mouth and lets The Mac put the vape to his mouth.

"Take a deep breath," The Mac says.

Bradley inhales then exhales.

"Another," says The Mac.

Bradley inhales and coughs.

"Another."

The Mac repeats this for every Neo on the line. X drops to one knee. His throat feels like it's closing and he can hardly breathe. He tries to stand but drops again from dysphoria. Whatever he smoked made him dizzy and weak in the knees.

"Stand up!" yells Machete.

Rodney rubs and covers his eyes. Jay Byrd stares into the ceiling with his mouth agape.

"You've just inhaled DimethylTryptamine, the spirit molecule," says Machete.

"We put the Psi in Psychedelics," said The Mac.

Destiny looks at her hands like she's never seen them before and then looks all around. She sees fractals all around the station as if everything is innately made of light. It looked like everything appeared to become painted glass like the ceiling and windows of a chapel. X felt dizzy but had a greater sense of everyone in the room. He felt the strongest sensation of how everyone and everything in all of creation was meant to be, it was faintly familiar to him. He looked around and noticed shapes within everything all interlocking together in a beautiful kaleidoscope or a puzzle that's been solved and would always be solved to him no matter the arrangement. Rodney felt this too, a bliss over his body. He felt as light as a feather and had thoughts about how much he loved being alive and how he knew God was watching over him.

"Yo what the fuck is this bruh, did yall see that?" Gerald suddenly whispers as he stared deep into the pit of darkness that swallowed the tracks.

"Shut up! We tell you when to talk!" yelled Machete.

The other Neos can't help but to also begin to focus on the darkness deep into the tunnels. Fear rushed over their bodies.

"We're about to see who they really are," said OG3 under his breath.

"Lock up!"

The Neos lock up single file with their arms locked underneath the under arms of the person in front like they had practiced in the room earlier. Gerald didn't lock up with the others. Instead, his legs wobbled and he collapsed. He crawls about the train tracks on his knees.

"Get up!" yelled OG3.

Gerald Screamed back.

"White Demon! White Devil! White Devil! Fucking White Devil!" Jay Byrd buried his eyes in Destiny's back for a moment forcing himself not to focus on the room which seemed to crawl and move, especially as they got deeper into the tunnel.

"Help! Help!" Gerald screams at the top of his lungs.

Machete unbothered looks at his watch then jumps down onto the tracks. He places blindfolds on the Neos and begins to speak.

"If his ass touch that back rail the electricity gonna fry his ass to death cuz I'm not pulling him off that shit. Oh yeah. It's real. You will die on line if you don't do what we tell you when we tell you." The Mac Jumps down to grab Gerald but Gerald kicked and fought at him and continued to scream.

"Don't touch me you white Devil!" screams Gerald.

"I got him, keep going!" The Mac exclaims.

"Let's go, march!" shouts OG3.

DMT has a weird ability to create a sensation that can frighten even the strongest person and bring latent fears to the fore. The chemical rushed through their veins creating an overwelming feeling of death and despair making them feel like they were beginning to melt into the environment. Like every single moment of their lives was a part of an intricate design and plot to lead them through the tunnels to die a very specific death. For a moment Bradley wished to himself while full of regret. Destiny's dose of DMT began to fill her with so much rage. Her perspective narrowed, prohibiting thoughts of life beyond the tunnel. X's heart was beating so hard he could barely hear. Jay Byrd closed his eyes and pushed the line forward.

"Follow my voice!" said OG3 in the near distance.

The line marched nearly 30 yards singing,

"I been training hard to be a Gamma
I been sentenced to
Omicron Rho
I been training hard to be a Gamma"
— *"Why?" yells Machete* —
"Because it is my will."

They traveled along the tracks stomping and twisting their bodies with violent force in every stomp and twist. The tracks beneath their feet began to rumble. X could feel his heart beating in rhythm with the stomping. It was like calling ordinary cadence but it felt deeper. Like what they were doing was rooted in the bones. Something older than everyone present.

"Stay together!" said OG3 with a distant voice.

"Unlock and we'll see y'all with the enlisted next year!" yelled Machete.

The tracks rumbled beneath their feet louder than before. A train was coming.

Suddenly OG3 yelled, "Get off the tracks!"

X's heart began to rush and beat even harder. Everyone on the line seemed to abruptly step in a separate direction. The train horn blared. The wheels of the approaching train screech in front of them.

"Get off the tracks!" OG3 yelled again.

The line went to move to the left and right simultaneously again. Their arms were locked in place. The entire line collapsed right on the middle of the tracks. It happened so quickly. They braced each other tightly as the roaring train fortunately was rushing by on the adjacent tracks. The entire line lay locked up on the ground, panicked and out of breath.

"Get Up!" yelled Machete.

They stood up catching their breath.

Machete removed the blindfolds.

"Yall would've fucking died...but y'all didn't unlock though... good. Continue."

The Neos continued to death march through the underground railroad following only a small light OG3 brandished up ahead.

"When the officers are too strong and the common soldiers too weak, the result is COLLAPSE. Sun Tzu, The Art of War," said Machete. Out of nowhere figures in black clothing appeared from the darkness and speared the line like angry bulls. They speared at the head and the tail. The line speared back. When the dark figures' efforts to collapse the line failed, they then yanked and jerked the Neos individually and pulled them away from the group to beat them in the dark until other Neos would come to aid. In every direction, dark figures. Warriors who had already become members of the CORR. Wave after wave the warriors emerged from the darkness and fought with strength that felt inhuman. The warriors held off as Bradley knelt at the front of the line struggling to catch his breath.

"Let's go Bradley, ya line need you! I'm not gonna tell you again," says Machete.

"I can't do this anymore," Bradley said.

"You take the front," he said to X. "

X knew they'd have a better chance with a fresh body in front and he was trained in battle already so he could probably take the oncoming warriors head on.

OG3 and Machete share a brief look.

"Y'all two switch," says OG3.

X and Bradley switch places on the line. X was now in the number 1 spot and Bradley the Number 2.

"Let's go," says OG3 as they march through the darkness.

The warriors again attacked the line from the front and the sides and the rear, this continued until the light of dawn.

"Five Neos left," Machete says, "there will always be a fight. Expect it from now on. If you're ready you won't have to get ready. In the words of the late Huey P. Newton, 'one of the first things any Black child must learn is how to fight well'…Go home Neos, you've got PT in an hour."

Later that day the Neos began several courses alongside the enlisted recruits. Critical Race Theory is one of the courses taught by Princess Ciara Leone within the Temple of New Karnak. The recruits sat in stairs of rows like at modern day universities with the professor at the bottom front and center.

Princess Leone spoke, "If you know the enemy and know yourself, your victory will not stand in doubt; Sun Tzu, the art of war. Here you all will learn about our true enemies from the structures and systems that perpetuate our destruction, to the people who sustain them. To know the systems in place against our people is key in discovering the true enemy's disposition today and throughout history. Today our fight is akin to guerrilla warfare. Our enemy hides among those unaware of the truth. Unaware or not they unknowingly attribute to the genocide of our people. If our enemy were to wear conventional uniforms, they would walk the streets of the upper wards sporting swastikas on their sleeves or white hoods over their heads with holes for their eyes. They've been embedded within our systems for centuries now. In every powerful entity they hide and embed themselves. At every level we grapple with agents of destruction and chaos and at the root…White supremacy. These agents of chaos were made comfortable by our very own government. Why? Because they wanted us extinct. Nazi scientists were imported from Nazi Germany around the time of WW2 under the justification of them being deemed necessary for the advancement of science and technology. Members of the socialist party responsible for the genocide of European Jews were allowed to work and live freely in the US and what they did with that freedom still haunts us and our bloodlines today. From 1939-1942 they implemented the Negro project and secretly deployed strategies that disproportionately affected melanated neighborhoods. The idea was to exterminate the melanated race through dismemberment of the family structure and the promotion of abortion at strategically placed planning parenting facilities which were publicly headed by eugenics enthusiast Margaree Singar but today we know the head of this organization to be much larger. Define eugenics? Anyone?" she asked.

No one raised a hand.

She notices Destiny asleep.

"Ms. Destiny Clarke."

A few students laugh.

"Wake her up," she commands.

One of the students sitting next to her wakes her up.

"Sleeping is for the barracks, not my class."

"Yes ma'am."

"If you're sleepy you may stand in the back of the class."

"I heard she played an amazing Jezebel spirit last night," murmurs the student behind Destiny named Aaron Hemingway who also goes by the name Aristotle.

A few of the others laugh.

"How about we step outside, and I break your jaw?" Destiny says with a straight face but stern tone.

"Young ma'am! Threats will not be tolerated in this classroom. Would you like to be removed and recycled?"

"No ma'am."

Destiny mugged Aristotle and turned to face forward. Princess Leone knew Destiny was tired from set the night prior but wouldn't allow her any excuse to sleep through class.

"Eugenics," Princess Leone continued, "the practice or advocacy of **controlled selective breeding of human populations** to 'improve the population's genetic composition. Margaree Singar and her colleagues believed that the Aryan race was the superior race and that all other inferior races were to be destroyed. They want us dead and that's the truth. Many outlets today will tell you a different story to protect their interests. We know the truth and we will never forget. This is how the system protects itself. Not much information has been left public about this matter, but we have a passage from a letter she wrote to Clarence J. Gamble, December 10th, 1939."

She waved her hand to command the smart board behind her to display a letter. It read.

"We don't want the word to go out that we want to exterminate the Negro population..."
— *Letter to Dr. Clarence J. Gamble, December 10, 1939, p. 2*

"We are waging a battle against a beast that has sought to destroy us for millennia," Princess Leone finished.

X and the other four recruits trained alongside the privates in the resistance during the day and as officers to be at night. They were learning everything from marksmanship, first aid and anatomy, land navigation, psychology of humans, and musical history. They even competed in intramural sports. During the nights they would train to fill their duties and responsibilities as officers learning everything from astrology, numerology, and battle strategies to the power of words and vibrations. Warriors in the CORR took up many roles in which they were assigned throughout training based on their strengths. Some were cooks, farmers, infantry, supply, intelligence, and more but no matter the job they all were taught self-defense and eventually to practice rapping daily. The vibrations and creation in real-time that was employed during free styling united the soul with the creator to slowly unlock the Godlike abilities within them.

"Why do I have to learn to shoot well when I'm just a farmer?" asked a recruit.

"It's better to be a warrior in a garden than to be a gardener in a war and stop shifting your finger on the trigger after every pull. Keep your finger's contact steady with the trigger," says T-Bone.

The enlisted recruits laid in their beds during the night while X and his line were training as neophytes. They were taught to call the night classes set. Set is named after the Egyptian God of war, chaos and storms and every night it was just that. Some nights OG3 would lead them, other nights The Mac or T-Bone would lead, and on the worse nights Machete would lead.

One cold rainy night, the Neos stand in a dark field shivering wet, tired, and exhausted.

"Let's hear it!" yells Machete commanding the Neos.

"To be a Gamma
You got to
You got to
You got to
say what you mean and
mean what you say
You got to say what you mean
And mean what you say

You got to
-Stomps rhythm in unison-
You got to
-Stomp-
You got to
-stomp-
You got to
"MORE ENERGY" OG3 screams. The line gets louder.
"To be a Gamma
You got to
You got to
You got toooooo
Say what you meannnnn and
Mean what you say
You got to
Say what you meannnnn and
Mean what you sayyyy
You got to
-stomp-
You got to
-stomp-
You got to"

They stomp then stop simultaneously at the position of attention.

"I almost felt a lor something moe, I'm not gon lie," says OG3, "You felt anything Machete?"

"Nah I ain't feel nothing," Machete replies.

Machete's towering, dark frame blends into the backdrop of the night.

"Y'all feeling it when yall say it?" asked OG3.

"Ain't no use in just saying shit just to be saying it, you gotta dig deep down in ya'll soul when you speak that, you gotta believe that!" Machete says.

"You gotta have E…enthusiasm, like this," says OG3.

He and Machete scrunch their faces up in the most contorted mug they could muster. With both of their fists at each of their sides they raised their chins in unison to the sky and yelled…

"To! Be! A! Gamma!

…

You got to!

Stomp*

(The ground trembled under their feet)

You got to!

-Stomp

(The ground shook with every stomp)

You got to!

-Stomp-

You got ta

say what you meannnnn!

and

mean what you sayyy!

You got to say what you meannnn!

And mean what you sayyyy!

You got to

-Stomp-

You got to

-Stomp-

You got to

-Stomp-

You gotstaa"

They stopped with a final stomp. The line stood with their eyes wide. Some even mouth agape as the ground beneath them finally settled. They had never seen anyone shake the Earth with just their feet before.

"And it's only 2 of us," said OG3, "No Excuses! Again!"

Every member of the line was mentally and physically worn down after weeks of burning the candle at both ends but their spirits and sense of purpose were sharper than they had ever been. They repeated new mantras and dances every day. The words and movements became a part of who they were. They strengthened their bonds and convictions and the words they spoke became their identity. The energy they forced through the words also was the force their bodies tuned into. The vibrations opened their throat chakra and progressed them toward the unlocking of their sacred abilities. The frequencies of the words they spoke were with pure enthusiasm. Every moving part of the line worked like the organs in the body. To work toward perfection and total unity is the great spiritual work and the spine of the curriculum of Locus The Great Father.

"When we pay attention to nature's music, we find that everything on Earth contributes to it's harmony."
-Hazrat Inyat Khan

CHAPTER 144.

MARVIN'S ROOM

Trevin Monroe was 17 years old living with his foster mom and his older brother Marvin in the south-side of Chicago. Trevin and his older brother were both born in the early 1970s and grew up during the crack epidemic and the start of gangster rap in the 80s. Trevin always watched when Marvin recorded on cassette tapes in his closet. He was always writing and rhyming.

"Wait till you hear my rhymes bro," said Trevin.

"Aight, gon' hit something real quick," Marvin replied.

"Nah big bro, you ain't ready for all that yet. When you get on my level, I got you," Trevin jokes.

Haha, Marvin laughed and said, "aight aight cool," as he pushed his little brother's head.

Rapping was something the kids at school would do every chance they could get. All the kids and teens from the neighborhood and local gangs would gather around in a circle as the bravest and coolest kids spit their rhymes after classes.

[Teen with the leather hat]
"I got soul
too cold for you to hold
switch the flow
you jive suckers don't know where to go
I got magic check the give and go
2 points fo' you even know
broke the fool like Geronimo
you too sweet like domino
penthouse wit the finest clothes
I be at where you find the hoes"

The crowd went crazy.

[Marvin]
"I been that you dumb alley cats

work jumping like jumping Jax
I got it covered baby just relax
you boys sweet like Scooby snacks
I'm the computer thought you knew the facts
she feeling me while I feel her sacks
I got her stuck like a cul-de-sac
she the center I'm the quarterback
that leather hat you should take it back
they want the flow like it's made of craaaack"

[Teen with the leather hat]
"You gon need a wish to be cool as me
peep the jewelry
fresh to death talking to the T
ain't nothing you can do with me
you in need of opportunity
I'm not with the tom foolery
you fooling them you ain't foolin me
you'll get burnt to the 3rd degree
I broke his chick she need surgery
Ya talk a lot you ain't hurtin me
I'm big Ace aint ya heard of me?"

"Ooohhh," some of the onlookers shout at various parts of each rap.

[Marvin]
"I aint no half stepper
he want the recipe but he too broke to buy the pepper
...
thinking he can step, he could never
I'm the type to flow to keep it going for forever
heavy handed p and you light like a feather

I'm stylin on ya crew yall gon have to work togetherrrrr
fly as me? Never
looking for me I could be wherever
probably somewhere mackin get licked like a letter
I took her from em strong arm da chick he ain't let her"

The two smiled at each other with mutual respect. Just then a fight broke out somewhere in the crowd and the crowd disrupted in panic. Marvin stood up on the steps to look over the crowd to see his little brother.

"Trev! Trev! Meet me cross the street!" yelled Marvin from above the rustling crowd.

Trevin made his way around the crowd to meet his brother. Marvin was making his way to the opening in the gate when someone in the crowd next to him ran up and tried to snatch his gold chain from around his neck. Marvin struggled with the teen.

The teen stabbed him in the gut then ran off. Trevin watched his brother try to hold on to the gate as he collapsed. Tragedy had struck the community. Marvin died from his wounds before the ambulance could arrive. No one spoke up about who was responsible. Trevin had lost his big brother and best friend and spent weeks in complete silence.

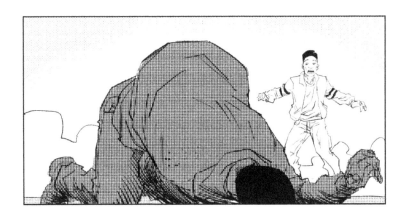

"You have to eat baby," said Trevin's mother as they sat at the kitchen table. Trevin twirled his fork in his peas.

A knock at the door breaks the silence. Trevin's mom goes and answers the door. It was Deandre, an older kid that used to record with Marvin.

"Hey Ms. Roundtree, how is he?" Deandre asked.

"Hey honey, he hasn't said a word since what happened to Marvin," she said.

"Well, here, I want him to have this. Marvin gave it to me, but he would have wanted him to have it."

"Thank you, sweetheart, I'll see that he gets it. Tell ya momma I asked about her for me, ok?"

"Alright."

She shut the door and walked back into the kitchen carrying with her a milk crate holding a dual tape recorder and about 10 tapes. She sat it at the table.

"Janet's boy dropped these off for you, he said Marvin would have wanted you to have it. You sure you don't want to talk?"

Trevin nodded yes. He looked at the tapes and saw the name of one of Marvin's songs. He grabbed the crate and ran up the stairs to

Marvin's room. He put the tape in the deck, rewound it, and pressed play.

(Tape clicks, beat plays)
[Marvin]
I'm too slick
I'm too nasty
Ya lady wanna have me
Tell her come get at me
Ima go getter
Harder than a rock
Boy I got soul all the way to my socks
Watch how I rock
might rock on ya block
or way up outer space
they want the juju I know they really want a taste
(The song continues…)

It had been a month since Trevin heard Marvin's voice. The tears swelled up in his eyes and ran down his face. He went through the rest of the tapes which were mostly beats until he went to bed in his brother's room. He lay wide awake thinking about his brother and the tapes. Usually, he'd have fallen asleep but tonight the energy in his body wouldn't even let him remain in bed. He got up and went into the closet like he watched his brother do so many times. He put one cassette inside deck number 1, pressed rewind, then put another into deck 2. He put the headsets on and pressed record…

[Trevin]

…

The beat played through, but Trevin couldn't find the words. Even though Trevin had spent a considerable amount of time practicing he just knew his big brother was much better than him. His posture sank and he wanted to disappear. He felt like he was letting Marvin down. Trevin remembered telling his brother how he'd rap for him one day. He knew he couldn't just give up; it wouldn't be right. He had to honor his brother, so he once again rewound the tapes, pressed play and record.

(The beat played)

[*Trevin*]
"Thinking bout my brother
don't know why this happened
I know if you was still here then you'd probably be rappin
talking bout mackin some ladies and I'd be laughing
Tryna, make it add up but the math aint really mathin
I swear to God I miss my brother I can't even lie
He always was a angel it's just now he in the sky
I used to want money but your life it can't buy
I look into the mirror don't een recognize the guy
pain in my chest
I can't even take it
I promise on my brother
that Ima still make it
my heart it aint there tell the truth it's really vacant
indebted to this thing I feel like I'm Ronald Reagan
You taught me keep it true and not to ever start faking
and time spent hating
could be love making
love was in ya heart

Enough to love Satan
Really tired of crying you would want me celebratin
I know you lookin down wanting to see me elevatin"

As Trevin rapped the hair on his head, arms, and neck began to stand up and the lights began to flicker.

[Trevin]
"I'ma represent the fam
I aint never stoppin
get up out the ghetto and go take momma shoppin
And always think about you every time I'm hip hoppin
we started out with nothing we aint lettin up or stoppin
and when I catch who killed you, we gon see his body droppin!
and when I catch who killed you, we gon see they body
dropping!"

Electrical sparks flowed around his body and he began to glow red as he repeated the words. The lights flickered off and on and the house began to shake.

[Trevin]
"And when I catch who killed you, we gon see they body droppin'!"
"Trevin!" his mother yelled.
"Brains on the floor ima hit that boy like Hopkins!" he yelled.
"Trevin!" she yelled again.

The tape popped out the deck, the music stopped, and Trevin seemed to come back to consciousness. He looked at his mom and she looked horrified at what she saw. Trevin looked afraid too, he also felt like he could lift a house.

The next morning Trevin and his mom really didn't talk or acknowledge anything from the night before. He went to school as he would a normal day. What Trevin and his mom didn't know was that the energy signature from his verse was big enough to generate a reading on the scanners of a covert government entity called the WTRD or World trade. The Weapons Technology and Research Division. They were created to ensure this country would always have access to the best available weapons and were constantly monitoring for usage of new ones. They had been developing technology to weaponize vibrations and music but hadn't been able to study anyone with such a unique gift close enough to gather research and to truly understand what it was. "Where did that reading come from? Who would have access to it in an underprivileged community?" They asked. Trevin's body was like an Earthquake mixed with an electro-magnetic pulse. The entire south-side and parts of Indiana experienced power outages. A military base in Rock Island had an outpost for the WTRD already monitoring for such occurrences. They were able to zero in on the general area but not exactly on who.

By the next evening they had raided every house on the block under the pretense of drug trafficking. They searched with their tools and instruments for the immense weapon but to no avail. Trevin had taken the tape with him to school unknowingly, helping his gift to remain a secret. When he got home his mother told him about the authorities searching everyone's homes and how scared she was for him.

"Baby, if the policeman stop you, it's yes sir, no sir. Don't talk back to him, just be quiet. Don't move unless they tell you to. They don't care about you. All they care about is they power and getting home," she said.

She kissed him on his head and rubbed his ears. "I have to go down to the church to help sister Sandra for the crab feast this weekend. I left dinner on the stove."

She left out and Trevin locked the door behind her. Trevin sat on the couch in the living room watching Inspector Gadget, but it didn't really hold his attention today. He wanted to understand what he felt during his freestyle but he didn't want to be the reason his mom would come back home to the house possibly destroyed. Maybe if I go outside, he thought. He was hungry for some snacks anyway so he grabbed enough change to buy some and headed out to the store. As Trevin walked, he could feel the rhythm of his breathing and the rhythm that he walked to in sync and began to rap to it.

[Trevin]
"Steppin' out late
thinking I'd escape
they want me stick to the script
like a played-out tape
too heavy for the fake
they can't be our weight

they just yelling from the bench they don't participate
step on a fool face make em dissipate
eatin' rappers like the food momma put on my plate"

Trevin could feel the sensation in his hair and skin again and this time in his feet. From inside a van up the block a white man watching a sonar-like device wearing headsets speaks into a mic.

"I'm picking something up out here. It's the same readings sir," the man says.

"Just keep a visual, you're the only unit for a few clicks out," a voice responded in the headset.

[Trevin]
"Boy ya breath stink get out my face
Ima super-fly mac from outer space
take ya chick and hit a route without a trace
keep a verb on my hip that's just in case"

The man in the van looks out the windshield.

"Sir it's coming from a Black kid," the man says.

"Say again, you've got a positive ID on that EMP?"

"Affirmative, it's the kid."

"Roger that, standby."

"What's a nigger think he's doing with a weapon like that?" says one of the two men in the van.

Trevin walks into the store. Everything appears brighter to him. He can feel the cashier looking at him and can sense the cashier's breathing. Everything is in rhythm flowing in harmony around him. From his blinking, his footsteps, even the door opening and closing behind him.

[Trevin]
"Playing suckers like the fiddle
I really been a mac ever since I was little"

"Can I help you?" the cashier asks in rhythm.

"Tea and some skittles
I only speak the truth
They think I'm speakin' in riddles."

"Huh?" asks the Cashier.

"Tea and skittles please. Thank you."

He hands the cashier the money, grabs his things, and exits the store. He feels like he could run a marathon, so much power running through his veins like he's never felt before.

"Sir he's moving pretty quick, we need to grab him now," says the man in the van.

"Negative, stand down units in route to your position."

"They always get away, screw this," he rips the headsets off, starts the van and heads after Trevin.

"Hey, come here!" one of them says as he hops out the sliding door of the approaching van.

He grabs Trevin by the arm and slams him against a wall.

"What're you think you're doing, boy?"

Trevin pushes the man up off his feet all the way back into the street. Trevin's eyes widened. He stares into his hands. He never felt strength like this before.

The man gets up.

"You son of a bitch!" he says as he charges Trevin again.

He knocks Trevin over and begins punching him. Trevin flips the man over and returns blows. He punches through the man's guard and knocks him unconscious.

"Freeze!" 4 shots are fired by the other man from the van into Trevin's back.

CHAPTER 233

Dawn has just arrived and the CORR recruits and Neos have gathered in the dining hall for breakfast. Heka, Heather, Machete and The Mac entered after everyone had taken a seat.

"Attention!" Someone calls out from among the recruits.

"At ease," Heka replies, "everyone take your seats. Here with us you will restore your connection with the Earth and with the source. Long Before colonization and mass fluoridation, our people primarily ate foods that derived from the Earth. We ate and gathered foods that were naturally high in energy that were not required to be heated, preserved, or processed."

Heather handed out apples to the recruits as they took notes.

"Thank you," said X with a grin.

"You're welcome," she replies, returning a smile.

Heka continues, "These heated, preserved, and processed foods tend to be almost exclusively acidic. Acidic foods create an acidic environment within the body which creates a substance called mucus. The main cause for disease. The default environment within a healthy body is an alkaline environment. Disease cannot live in an alkaline environment. Here are some foods that detox and remove mucus from the body. Seeded melons, key limes, mangoes, sea moss, onions, leafy greens, ginger, and oranges. These foods were the ingredients during times of healing. Ginger root for vomiting and menstrual cramps. Chamomile flowers for cuts, scrapes, and rashes."

They passed around examples of the herbs that were spoken of. Heather sat down next to X.

Heka continues, "this is ginger. It has incredible health benefits. It fights against cold and flu, can lower blood pressure, relieve cramps, protect you against cancer and speed up one's metabolism."

They passed around ginger so everyone could see.

"Ever tried ginger?" Heather whispers to X.

"I don't think so," he replied.

"Go on," she says.

He bites into the ginger and immediately scrunches up his face then sticks out his tongue.

"Ughh, it tastes sting-e."

"Sting-e?" Heather burst out a laugh…

"Alright keep it down, you two," Heka continues, "Peppermint leaves were used to rid the body of nausea, congestion, and gas. Lavender for stress and anxiety and minor burns. I really get excited about healing the body. Did you know the colors of the food directly correspond with the activation of the chakra that's the same color? No? You might want to jot that down. I think that's enough food for thought for now. I'm hungry. Put your notebooks away and let's eat," he says as he smiles and scratches his head.

Plates full of fruit were passed around for the new recruits to eat for breakfast. OG3 sat with Heather and the other 4 Neos.

"I wonder what they're eating in the upper wards," asks Bradley.

"Only the best I've heard," said X.

"I mean if you consider karmic filled acidic meats the best," said Heather. X chuckles.

"The streets are paved with gold is how the story goes," says OG3.

"Where everyone has running water and a place to lay their heads.

Where they enjoy weekends full of virtual golf, mansion parties, orgies, electric cars, and brunches on rooftops."

"Sound alright to me," Bradley joked.

"Yea right," said Rodney.

"What made you join the CORR?" Rodney asked OG3.

"I was born among the CORR. My mother and father served. I couldn't imagine doing anything else," he replied.

"Machete brought you in?" asked Jay Byrd.

"Yeah, once I got of age. Machete, Heka, and T-Bone were some of my Prophytes too," said OG3.

"I never got to ask, why they call you Jay Byrd?" Bradley asked.

"My mother. She always said I was gone end up in and out of jail like a jail bird cuz of the stuff I was into," Jay Byrd replied.

"What you was into?" asked Rodney.

"...nothing I'm into nomore. Somebody had to feed us. Damn sure wasn't my folks," he replied.

"Haha ya mom gave you that name? It be ya own people," said Bradley.

"Like shit," Jay Byrd replied

"Better than my mom. I never even knew her. She aint even want me. Gave me to the government," said X.

"Nah, who told you that?" asked OG3.

"Learned it in the camps," X replied.

"Everything you learned over that jawn you might as well scratch. Unlearn and relearn," OG3 said, "ya mom didn't know they would keep you trust me, nobody did. They started that program promising a longer life for Blacks. Saying stuff like the procedure would give us hope, which it did. When Project Black Beam first started transitioning them children in the 70s, they would give y'all back to the families and allow y'all to protect the neighborhoods y'all came from. But eventually, like 20 years later in 2093 a few years after Project Black Beam became law, they just straight kept y'all at them child camps. They say y'all had a greater chance of survival in there. It's really cuz the first of y'all was getting in they asses every time some bullshit popped off if you ask me. Y'all used to fight for us. Smashin' on crooked cops, Neo Nazi muh fuckas', and organ traffickers, but they don't tell y'all that forreal."

CHAPTER 377

Late in the afternoon the recruits fill the seats to study human anatomy and physiology. Princess Leone aims the red laser pointer at a diagram depicting human skeletons. One male, the other female.

"As we can see depicted here the male shoulders are typically wider and higher. Below we have the female's thorax which is typically narrower. Can anyone point out any other differences?" She asks. Destiny raises her hand.

"Yes ma'am," says Princess Leone as she points to Destiny.

"The female pelvis is wider than the males to facilitate the natural birth of everyone ever," says Destiny.

Some classmates laugh.

"Correct, anyone else?" Princess Leone replied.

Aristotle who sat behind Destiny comments, "That all yall any good for?"

A few snickers of laughter break out before Princess Leone Interjects, "Excuse me Mr. Hemingway is there something you'd like to add to the discussion?"

"No Princess Leone," he replied.

"I didn't think so," she replied sharply, "I heard what you said. misogyny has no place in the CORR. You have much to learn. As if bringing life into the known world wasn't enough. When Imperial forces of Italy arrived at the borders of Ethiopia it was Tatyu Betul, wife of Emperor Menelik who led 6,000 strong to victory in war against the Italians to retain Ethiopia's sovereignty. The only nation in Africa to successfully thwart colonization. Women made up about half of the Black Panther party membership and often held leadership roles. Throughout history melanated women have proven more than worthy of respect. How dare you sit in front of your peers and speak in such a distasteful manner? If I hear anything else like that, you'll have me to deal with. In the words of Dr. Angela Davis when Black women stand up, as they did during the Montgomery Bus Boycott, as they did during the Black liberation era, Earth-shaking changes occur. Don't be the reason I stand up Mr. Hemingway."

Destiny scratches the back of her shoulder with her middle finger toward him.

"Do I make myself clear?" Princess Leone says sternly.

"Yes ma'am."

Jay Byrd raised his hand.

"Jaleel," says Princess Leone.

"Why are we learning about the differences between male and females? What difference does it make?"

"Good question, the core of your training and purpose here in the CORR is to know yourselves and your enemies extensively. Inside and out. You'll be surprised at how handy our subconscious can truly be when given the proper tools. Plus, some of your fellow classmates haven't previously undergone anything similar to a traditional education and need to be properly introduced to the human body. Gotta know this stuff or people will try to tell you anything. Can anyone else identify any notable differences other than the ones previously stated? I want to see who's been studying." One of the males in the class raised his hand.

"Deion," she says.

"The Adam's apple!"

"What about it?"

"Males have one and women don't."

"Almost, we have them as well; they just don't grow as large as our male counterparts, the scientific term is the laryngeal Prominence. This is also the gate to the throat chakra, which a few of you have managed to open I hear. Very inspirational, keep up the good work and for those who haven't, don't fret your time will come. I look forward to seeing you all unlock your first 7."

"Your highness," Rodney says as he raises his hand.

"Yes, Mr. Reynolds."

"The text only mentions 7 chakras."

"Yes, but there are many more. Some of the greatest warriors we have, have unlocked far more than 7. Complete your training and the strengths you acquire from the opening of your Chakra will be yours to use at will."

"Well, how many are there?"

"You should only concern yourselves with the 7 we teach you for now."

Another recruit raises their hand.

"Yes, Quentin?"

"Is this the God tongue?" he asks.

Princess Leone paused for a moment.

"Yes, our elders and prophets tell us the time of the legendary God tongue is near. Where there will be one among us who creates as they speak. One who will wield superhuman abilities as we've never seen before. The sublime glow. The one who will free us."

LATER THAT EVENING BACK AT AMARA...

The clergy and high-ranking officers of Amara meet in the council's chamber to discuss newly discovered intel.

"Take your men and get this to the other colonies immediately," King Anthony says.

A warrior of the CORR enters the chamber.

"Sir, augmented squads are storming complexes nearby. We've got units ready to take them out. Awaiting your orders," he says.

"Sire, we can take them out and make our way to New Karnak," says Heka.

"Alright, keep your heads down and relay the information. Stay off the comm's as much as you can," the King replies.

Heka bowed and turned to face the warrior who entered.

"On me," Heka says.

He and 8 other warriors exit from a hidden bunker-like entrance within Amara. About 100 or so feet away was a military convoy parked outside an old factory they used to make and store clothing in the lower wards.

"Let's move," says Heka.

They close in on the convoy and take cover nearby.

"UAV up ahead sir," says one of the warriors in Heka's squad.

"We can't do anything with it hovering like that. Switch to direct-energy munitions and prepare to take it out," says Heka.

4 augmented Black soldiers from the military units exit the front door of the old factory. One of the soldiers is dragging 2 women

by their hair and drops them in the center of the convoy. 5 soldiers stand and watch as the 2 women are forced to their knees execution style.

"Take out the two with therm o-vision first on my mark," says Heka.

17 is one of the soldiers raiding the factory. He walks and stands in front of the two kneeling women. He uses his pistol to raise one of their chins to establish eye contact.

"Tell me where the bad guys are," he says.

"It doesn't matter what you do, the prophecy has come to fruition. Your ignorance and darkness will be obliterated," says the woman. 17 laughs.

"Oh, she talkin' about their Dalai Lama! You talking about your Dalai Lama? Where is he exactly?" 17 asks with a smile.

Some of the soldiers laugh.

"Y'all dumb as shit believing in that mumbo jumbo," one of the augmented soldiers said.

"The God tongue lives, whether you believe or not," she says.

17 laughs.

"How about I show you my God tongue?" he says and sticks out his tongue.

She spits. He shoots the other woman in the face.

"Last chance," he says sharply.

His smirk is now gone. He puts the hot barrel to her cheek. Shots ring out in the distance. The bullets whip close to 17. The two augmented soldiers with the Thermo -vision get hit and drop. 17 and the others duck and take cover near the trucks. The UAV that hovered overhead crashed into a nearby building.

"Where's it coming from?" 17 yells.

A dense white smoke begins to cover the convoy. Bullets ricochet off the vehicles and the trading of fire continues. 17 sees rebel warrior boots running toward the convoy beneath all the smoke. He shoots a few of their feet and ankles. Heka then grabs 17 by the back of 17's vest, picks him up, and slams him on his back. 17 hits the ground with a loud thud. Heka punches at him. 17 blocks while still on his back and kicks Heka's feet causing his legs to be swept from underneath him. Heka falls on top of 17. They roll around until 17 kicks Heka off him. 17 shoots blasts from his man cannon in his arm, but Heka rolls and takes cover behind one of the armored vehicles. 17 drops to the floor to look for Heka's feet to shoot but Heka's feet were gone. He looks up to see Heka standing on top of the vehicle. Heka fires 2 rounds from a pistol into 17's head.

BACK AT NEW KARNAK...

Later that night the Neos depart from the enlisted recruits and warriors for set. They meet up in the woods a few miles away from the colony.

"Line up," commands Machete.

They lined up in height order with firm postures.

"Let's go!"

Each member was given a cinder block painted with their specific number corresponding with their placement on line during the process and were expected to keep it with them during set. They each pick up their blocks and begin to jog in a single file.

"5 miles this time, 1 for each of you. Every time we have to stop cuz one of y'all need a break, that's 25 cinder-squats," Machete orders. "You know the drill number one *(referring to X)*, we're going directly north so just keep track of the Polaris."

He begins calling playful cadence, "Left, Yo left, yo left right… Yo left."

The recruits get in step. Machete continues the cadence. They repeat his words in unison.

[Machete calls and the Neo's respond]
"When my granny was 91
When my granny was 91
She pledge Gamma just for fun
She pledge Gamma just for fun
When my granny was 92
When my granny was 92
She pledge Gamma better than you
She pledge Gamma better than you
When my granny was 93
When my granny was 93
She pledge Gamma better than me
She pledge Gamma better than me
When my granny was 94
When my granny was 94
She pledge Gamma more and more
She pledge Gamma more and more
When my granny was 95
When my granny was 95
She pledge Gamma to stay alive
She pledge Gamma to stay alive
When my granny was 96
When my granny was 96
She pledge Gamma doing flutter-kicks
She pledge Gamma doing flutter-kicks
When my granny was 97
When my granny was 97
She up and died and went to heaven
She up and died and went to heaven
She met Snoop Dogg at the pearly gates
She met Snoop Dogg at the pearly gates
Said, "Snoop, O Snoop hope I'm not late

Said, "Snoop, O Snoop, hope I'm not late
Snoop Dogg *said with a big ol' grin*
Snoop Dogg said with a big ol' grin
"Get down granny, and knock out ten"
"Get down granny, and knock out ten"
She replied with a big ol' smile
She replied with a big ol' smile
"Sorry, Snoop Dogg, I'm on profile!"
"Sorry, Snoop Dogg, I'm on profile!"

They ran and yelled cadences for the next 30 minutes.

"Squad Halt," says Machete.

The recruits stop running and begin to catch up on their breathing.

"5 Cinder Squats lets go!" They raise the cinder blocks above their heads, squat, and count 5 squats.

"5 miles here 5 miles back. From now on, I want the number 5 to forever be cemented into your minds. There are now 5 of you and should always be 5 of you. That is your number. You must understand that 5 is a very powerful number and it is no coincidence that it is now a part of you. There are not more than five musical notes in the pentatonic scale, yet the combinations of these five give rise to more melodies than can ever be heard. There are not more than five primary colors, yet in combination they produce more hues than can ever been seen. There are not more than five cardinal tastes, yet combinations of them yield more flavors than can ever be tasted. There are no more than 5 senses, yet they come together to provide us with the euphoric experience of life. From this moment, this line is to forever be known as the 5 heartbeats. Though this number may appear minor against our foe, you 5 will rise against them and your success will stand as a testament of God's favor to our people."

Just then Machete looked over his shoulder with great concern.

"We have to go…follow me."

They head back into the direction they came with great haste. X couldn't put his finger on it, but something was wrong. No cadence or drills, just an all-out sprint back home. A deep galloping could begin to be heard in the distance.

"Keep running," orders Machete.

The galloping continued, becoming close to their rear. Closer and closer the loud galloping got no matter how fast they seemed to run.

"Drop the cinder-blocks," says Machete.

"But," Destiny replied.

"Drop the cinder-blocks!" Machete yells.

The loud galloping continued. Everyone dropped their blocks. To the far right off the side of the mountain below trees were snapping and crashing at the same rate as they ran. Machete stops and stares in the direction of the loud galloping and crashing and yells for the others to keep going.

They ran about 100 yards before Jay Byrd stopped to look back. The others stop to look as well. *Goom, goom, goom, goom, goom**

The loud galloping continues and finally slows until it stops. Out of the darkness stand a four-legged Mech standing as tall as the trees with a red light above a turret. The red light scans Machete then scans up ahead. Machete turns his head to see the others still in the machine's view.

"Hey! Focus on me you worthless piece of scrap metal!" yells Machete.

The Mech walks slowly toward Machete and stops. Beeping sounds emanate from the Mech. Machete mugged the Mech and positioned his feet to get a firmer stance.

*Click, Brrrrrt**

The Mech's turret began to spray a constant barrage of bullets at Machete. Machete dodged to the left as dust clouds filled the air from the bullets hitting the ground. X and the other Neos eyes widened as they had never seen a person move so fast.

"He needs our help," says Destiny.

Brrrrrrrt*

The Mech continues to fire and misses Machete. Machete sprints off to the left then to the right and then like a train, spears the Mech in it's side knocking it off it's feet. He quickly climbs atop the Mech and punches through the frame that housed the red light and crushes what was inside. Smoke and broken glass spray around his hand. Machete looks up to see his recruits staring in amazement.

"Get out of here, more will zero in on this one's position any moment now!"

They take off running.

"Did you fucking see that?" asks Bradley.

"I didn't know he could move that fast," Rodney says.

"I didn't know anybody could move that fast," X replied.

Goom goom, goom goom, goom, shhhhh*

Another Mech slides down the side of the mountain just up ahead of where they are heading. X pauses, plants his feet, and charges the weaponry in his right arm as it reconstructs itself into a cannon.

Brrrrrrrrrrrt*

The Mech shoots wildly in the direction of the Neos. X returns fire from his cannon into the direction of the Mech but misses. They traded fire back and forth. X gets a charged blast to hit which blows one of the legs out from under the Mech, but it still was able to fire at them from a tilted position.

"I'm gonna draw his fire, you just get that shot!" orders Destiny.

"Wait!" says X.

He could feel the heat from the bullets whizzing near his face. His heart was pumping in his throat. She darted out in the open gaining the Mech's attention then dodged back behind cover. X was frozen. He missed the moment. He couldn't understand how she was able to risk her life in the heat of confrontation with this powerful machine. Even with no weaponry of her own. Just then Machete sprinted up to the vulnerable side of the Mech and punched a hole through the Mechanism with the red light forcing his fist through the frame disabling it.

"Let's move!" orders Machete.

Through the darkness of night, they make their way back to the colony. Heka sat on the steps waiting for them with a small squad of CORR warriors.

"Lieutenant!" said Machete to Heka.

"Captain," said Heka. "We have important matters to discuss."

"Go to the barracks and await orders," Machete says to the Neos.

"I know it's bad if you here this late," he says to Heka.

Machete and Heka head into a conference room.

"Intel has identified a new threat to our people," Heka says.

"Wouldn't be 4 legged turrets, would it?" said Machete.

"Close…but worse. An entire army of them with several different fleets of powerful machinery controlled by a singular software. Ships, androids, and even neural linked soldiers... the next generation"

"Neural linked?"

"Yes, free will wiped, no fear, no conscience."

"Where are they coming from?"

"Intel's been digging up everything they can find, hacking databases and pulling strings on our inside guys. A weapons manufacturing company with Neo Nazi puppets running the show, 'Aerotech'. They've been contracted by the military. They're ordering up a bunch of hardware somewhere east. They've been working the kinks out of the new AI we've been hearing about, and it's been giving us hell down south."

"How often yall rubbing paint with 'em down there?"

"We're seeing 8 incidents a week; they know we're there now and their funneling fire and forces in our AO. It's only a matter of time until they possibly find us."

"What's the plan?"

"Our top guys are developing a bug for the software named Scarab to decommission the AI, hopefully we can get it operational soon."

"Ok, so what brings you here? Evac?"

"The AI attacks our firewall over a million times…daily. We can't thwart every attempt and don't want to risk the AI getting whiff of our communications. The admirals and clergy here and at Amara have already been briefed on the situation and any current protocol moving forward. Go dark and perform tasks as analog as possible to remain operational. Until we can deploy the bug, remain within the walls unless absolutely necessary, they're swarming the regions near some of the colonies."

"What's the upper wards saying about this?"

"They're already switching a large portion of their security forces over to the AI, as for the battles in the lower wards they're still blaming rap extremists and local militia forces," Heka replies.

"Sheep," Machete replies.

Inside the barracks the others have already begun to discuss the AI.

"They don't want to do their own dirty work, so they programmed the computers to come for us," says one of the recruits.

"We just gotta wait it out," Bradley replies.

"All I know is I ain't stepping outside without some heat again, we almost got ripped to shreds by that thing," says Jay Byrd.

"You guys fought a Mech out there?" one of the recruits asks.

"Yea we almost didn't make it back," Jay Byrd replied.

"Yea but Machete wasn't gonna let that happen."

"He was moving faster than the bullets," said X.

"What? No way he's almost 300 pounds," one of the recruits added.

"He's telling the truth," Destiny adds. "We all saw it with our own eyes, I could barely see his movements and he punched right through the metal frame."

"He's been training for over a decade, I've heard he's one of the ones who used rap to unlock a bunch of chakra," one of the recruits said.

"Yea well, we gonna unlock ours too. He was like a God or something! If I could move like that, I'd kill every last one of them White devils in the upper wards with my bare fricken hands!" Destiny exclaims.

"That is precisely why your abilities remain embryonic and rudimentary," says Heka as he and Machete enter the bay.

"Attention!" someone in the room yells and all the recruits stand and seize chatter.

Heka walks toward Destiny boots tapping against the marble in the silence.

He then continues to speak, "We do not kill based off race alone. We do not kill indiscriminately. That would be to perpetuate in the world that in which we wish to change. We are not our enemies. Everything in this realm serves a purpose. From the most distant star in the sky to the microorganisms mating on our faces. To the cosmos you and I are no different than the ants in the hill to us," he says as he finally stands face to face with Destiny and then walks away.

"Everything we can touch, hear or smell is living and vibrating. Sending and receiving messages just like you and me. We're all the same. Everything living deserves life. Free your minds of revenge and encourage your brothers and sisters to do the same if you wish to see them become their best selves. Your growth will surprise you one day."

Destiny lowers her head.

"Do not lower your head, remain proud. We are a proud race of people. I was told of your heroics today…You all risked your lives for each other. Something I could not understand in my youth.

At ease… when I was a child, my mother was killed by the Rap Enforcement Administration during a no-knock raid. I could not process this. I was a child full of rage. Lost and alone. It was the CORR that found me as a small boy and took me in. Still, I remained upset with my mother for many years for dying and leaving me alone.

I could not understand her sacrifice until the late Charles Brown, one of my Prophytes said to me, "We may not have gotten the choice whether to be brought into this world or not, but sometimes we do get to choose what's really worth leaving it for."

The room was still. It was quiet enough to hear an ant sneeze.

He continued, "Many years later I would come to realize my mother's sacrifice in a greater capacity once I watched others like myself be taught to forgive and use the dark times as motivation and achieve incredible feats using rap as the outlet to do so. The very thing my mother was killed trying to protect. Without it I wouldn't be here with you today. The path of rage and revenge would have destroyed me and possibly countless others. That's why if you wish to be your most powerful selves each and every one of you will also need to develop your own ability to rap," Heka paused. The room remained silent as the young warriors reflected on what was said.

Then Machete began to speak, "We've arranged for each of you to begin attending private lessons with the Chaplain so that you may experience your gifts as well."

"What's a Chaplain?" Rodney asks.

Heka again began to respond.

"The Chaplain is the clergyman or religious liaison for the unit so to speak. You will be meeting him momentarily. Every unit of the CORR has their own. He or she is expected to be exceptionally skilled and versed at "off the dome rapping" to achieve strength beyond that of a normal human. Every Chaplain is said to have achieved oneness with the creator at some point and have unlocked at least 7 chakras. We often refer to them as beings of light. They are here to personally guide us."

"How do y'all know for sure they unlocked them?" asked Destiny.

"They're verified by the ones among us who have the ability to read auras and once a person unlocks a certain amount of chakra it's undeniable even to the lowest vibrating entities," Heka replied.

"So, I mean, what are we supposed to throw hands with words?" Destiny sarcastically asks.

"Destiny!" Rodney whispers sharply.

"It's alright," says Heka. "What you're referring to is battle rap, and yes."

"Battle rap?" asks Destiny.

"Yes," said Heka with a smile, "Get good enough at that and your hands will never need to be thrown."

"Good evening," says the Chaplain as he enters the room. He is dressed in a black thobe with honors on the Left breast and a major's rank.

"Good afternoon, I am Major Jordan but to many I simply go by The Chaplain," he exclaims.

"Each of you for an hour a week will be sent to me. We will be developing your rapping abilities: flow, rhyme scheme, confidence, tone, and deliveries. I can sense a lot of you are nervous and harbor insecurities, it's ok and quite normal actually," he says with a smile.

"If you are feeling any pressure to be a certain level, don't. Some will excel, some won't."

X clenches his jaw; he can barely hide his facial expression.

"Oh, I sense some of you are eager to achieve this," says Major Jordan.

"Rapping is sort of like intercourse. Humanity needs it. Everyone can achieve it, some do it in a group. Some record it. Some wait until marriage."

"Sir!" Interjected Machete.

"Oh relax captain. Some of you will find your natural talents are in other elements of hip hop. You all familiar with the elements from class?"

"Ahh no, we don't introduce them to that until later in the curriculum," Machete replies.

"Ugh, I guess I'm old school. Haha," Major Jordan responds.

"Yea we doin' things a bit different this year, case by case basis. The five elements are emceeing, deejaying, breaking, graffiti, and beatboxing will be introduced to you when we believe you all are ready on an individual level," Machete replies.

"My first student will be Reese. So please accompany me to the other room," Major Jordan announces.

Major Jordan, Reese, Heka and Machete left the room.

"He doesn't seem so strong to me," Destiny says.

"You couldn't feel that?" Bradley asks.

"Feel what?"she asks.

"I don't know, it's like he was on a different level," said Bradley.

"I could feel it too," added another recruit.

"Y'all falling for that spooky crap. Well, I ain't buying till I see him throw hands," said Destiny.

"He's right," Jay Byrd added as he sat on his bed in the recessed wall. "Don't be so quick to judge. I could feel it too. He was rhyming his words since he walked in the room."

X quietly gasped.

"Yall didn't even notice," said Jay Byrd.

"He was not," said Destiny.

"He was. I wouldn't underestimate this, Chaplain," said Jay Byrd.

Machete walks back into the bay.

"Attention!" one of the soldiers yelled.

Everyone stood up and got quiet.

"You 5 let's go," said Machete.

The Neo's follow him into the armory.

"Seems like you 5 have a hard time hearing. I told you all to get out of there back when those Mech units showed up, and yall wanted to stand around. You owe me 250 Cinder-squats each."

"But we dropped our Cinder-blocks sir," said Destiny.

"Oh, that's right ain't it? Each of you grab one of those 5-gallon water bottles over there... yea that should do it."

"Ugh," they all groan.

Machete smiles.

"It'll be the same ones that smoke wit ya,"
-A Poet 1994

610.

"The Recruits begin their work with the chaplain this week, sire," says Ali who serves as King Yahweh's courtier.

"They need to cross soon," says King Yahweh.

"We can only cross them when they are ready sire," says Machete.

"We don't have the privilege of time enough for pomp and circumstance, Captain," King Yahweh responds.

"But the God tongue sire, it cannot be rushed. We must not disturb it's process. If one of the recruits possesses it as La Sirene prophesied this war will soon be over."

"It could very well come from any one of us, I have yet to hear or see anything impressive from this group to believe it is coming from them."

"There's no way to know yet your majesty. We have yet to witness any real flow or engineering from them."

"Then I'll hear no more of this until we've received word from Chaplain Major Jordan."

MEANWHILE AT THE SCHOOLHOUSE...

Can anyone tell me what significant event in history happened regarding our people in the year 2043?" asks T. Bone.

A recruit raises her hand.

"Yes Mabel."

"Blacks in the United States had received reparations for chattel slavery and discriminatory practices from the federal government."

"Correct! $20,000 and free college for every Black citizen in the States," T Bone replies.

He then adjusts himself in his seat in preparation to ask another question.

"Can anyone tell me what the issue was with that? No one? We agreed to this during a time where we were the least organized, the value of a college degree declined as well as the value of the dollar. Popular currencies traded throughout the world at the time were decentralized. The reparations melanated people agreed on essentially had no value."

The Chaplain enters the room.

"Alexander," the Chaplain called out. X grabbed his things with great urgency and headed down the hall with the Chaplain. It was time for his first private lesson.

SCAN FOR MORE CONTENT AND TO UNLOCK ADDITIONAL
CHAPTERS

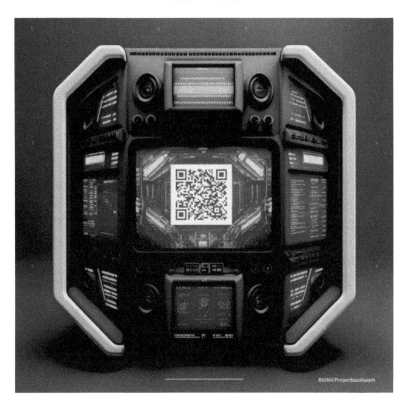

The hour had completely passed and the needle began to track the dead wax near the middle of the record. A low-level white noise repeated as the record spun. X reached out to the record player.

"How was it?" asked the Chaplain as he walked in the room.

"It's crazy, he could talk about his life in rhythms and rhymes like magic or something," X replied as his hand returned to his side.

"You could really understand his story huh?" the Chaplain said while lifting the needle.

"Yes sir, guess I could kind of relate."

"Stereotypes of a Black male misunderstood, yeah..." said the Chaplain. X smiled and nodded his head in agreement.

EARLIER THAT DAY
AT AEROTECH OPERTIONS CORPORATION...

"Those two downed Roamers from the other day. Where were they?" asked Christine Rivers, CEO of Aerotech.

"Unit 88 and 106…Those were destroyed in District 6 Nevada ma'am," replied the analyst.

"The lower wards...do we have surveillance feed?" she asked.

"Yes Ma'am," the analyst replied.

"Pull it up."

"Focus on me you worthless piece of scrap metal."

Brrrrrrrrt* - *crashing noises finally static*

"Whoa did you see that?" said one of the analysts.

"No way," said another.

The room erupts in conversation.

"Silence. Play it again," said Christine.

Footage plays back

*"Focus on me you worthless…."

"Pause it," Christine says. "Run him through the database. I wanna know who he is. Show me the other one."

***Brrrrrt gisssst brrrrt giiiist*, footage plays**

"Pause it…that's Lockhart technology."

"Run his metrics as well and get this over to Lockhart now."

"Yes ma'am."

"I want every available unit loaded and ready to canvas every square inch of that District."

"Yes ma'am."

MEANWHILE BACK AT NEW KARNAK...

Back at New Karnak King Yahweh called a meeting with his council and high-ranking officers.

"The AO is getting too hot right now. Our Men are engaging small arms squads near the temple in greater numbers than ever recorded. I propose we vote on enacting operation Pacific Rim," said Andre Benjamin III.

"They're already on top of us. How do you propose we just up and move everything undetected?" asked Machete.

"We jump right to phase 3," Andre Replied.

"And leave everything we built? No, we stay and fight," Curtis replied.

"If we don't leave, we may very well be destroyed along with everything we've built," Andre explained.

"You should know better than to curse us with your tongue in such a manner," said Princess Leone.

"I only speak from the sincerity of my heart, your highness," Andre replied.

"And when we get to the shores, when will we stop? Or do you plan to cower into the depth of the oceans as well?" asked Curtis.

"No, there we fight with our backs to the ocean. The last stand," Andre replied.

"I find no solace in running with our pants down to go fight on the edge of the pacific," said Curtis, "we mustn't let our children become as our fathers, beggars to live in someone else's home."

"We will vote," Princess Ciara Leone declared.

"All in favor of initiating operation Pacific Rim. Raise your right hand," she said.

Most of the room raised their hands.

"Put them down. All opposed?"

Some council members raise their hands.

"King Yahweh, you do not wish to vote?" asked Princess Leone.

The King sucked his fingers free of the flavor from the chicken he is eating and after a final swallow began to speak.

"Interesting, the chaplain has voted in favor of cutting and running in the night…have you not found our savior among the new recruits?" The Chaplain waited for a moment.

"No," he replied. Chatter and confusion flood the room.

"Quiet down, Quiet down," said one of the advisors.

"Your majesty, I need more time with them," said the Chaplain.

"He needs more time with them," he chuckled. "We will stay and fight. We've remained hidden for this long. Let us not just abandon ship, yes?" said King Yahweh.

"The king has spoken," said Ali.

"You have 14 days then you will cross the Neos and graduate the new recruits. We'll need all the manpower we can get," said the King

"We must cross them when they are fit to battle your majesty," Machete replied.

"The King has spoken!" yelled one of the council members.

"The next outburst from you will be recognized as civil disobedience, which might I remind you is a punishable offense, Captain," said Ali to Machete.

Machete took deep breaths as he clenched his fists and jaw in silence.

The King smiled and continued to eat.

"We will stay here and fight," said the King. Indeed, he had said a mouthful.

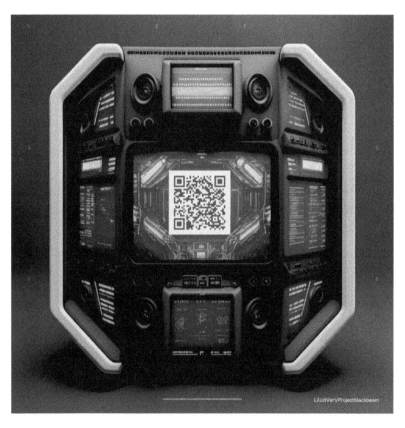

SCAN FOR MORE CONTENT AND TO UNLOCK ADDITIONAL
CHAPTERS

CHAPTER 987

The recruits sit in class and listen as T-Bone explains colonialism and some of the negative effects it has on melanated people.

"Wait, so you're saying that European nations actually removed the features from the monuments once they took control of those countries?" asked Jaleel.

"Correct, that's exactly what I'm saying. The removal of noses and Africanoid features from monuments and relics was to aid in destroying your connection to the most sought-after civilizations in history. Till this day, you had no idea you were related to these beautiful, royal, and intelligent people," T-Bone explains as images of royal Africans projected in 3 dimensions.

"I love being Black," said Rodney.

"That's another thing. Keep from identifying yourself as that as much as possible," T-Bone replies

"Why? I'm Black," Rodney replied.

"The term Black only exists in America and under American influence. What did they call white people in other countries?" T-Bone asks.

No one answered.

"Americans, they called us all Americans…not White or Black. The term Black originated in America once plantation owners needed to find reasons to keep people indentured to servitude indefinitely. They needed a reason to separate the people. A reason to justify us as different and inhuman. To profit. So you became Black and they became White. Ever heard an Asian American refer to themselves as yellow? Or Hawaiians as orange or some other color? No, they refer to themselves as where they are from."

"Attention!" A recruit calls out as the Chaplain entered the room.

"You don't see me in the room? Really? Do push ups till I tell you stop," says T-Bone to the recruit who called the Command.

"Please continue T-Bone," said the Chaplain.

"Yes, they refer to themselves in a way that connects them to a nationality. We have been stripped of who we are and labeled as an adjective. You're not even recognized as a person when you identify that way."

"I'm just American?" asks Rodney.

"Yes, but when we are equipped to live freely above ground you will be referred to as Amarian since you were born in the Kingdom of Amara. How may I help you Chap?" T-Bone then asks.

"I'm here for Alexander," the Chaplain says. X grabs his things and heads to the recording and listening room with the Chaplain.

"How's training going?" asks the Chaplain.

"Everybody's pretty worked up about the AI to be honest, we just wondering when the fighting gonna start again," X replied.

"Well, take solace in the fact that no AI is as complex and powerful as what's in here," says the Chaplain as he points to his head.

"Yes sir." They enter the room.

"Go on, same as last time."

X looked at the shelves packed with Vinyl covers. There were all sorts of colors to choose from that caught his eye.

X closed his eyes, ran his hand across the record covers and grabbed one.

"The Goat," said the Chaplain.

X opens his eyes to read the album cover; it reads Polo G 'The Goat' and a signature on the bottom left corner.

"Pick a different one," the Chaplain orders.

"Why?"

"You need an advanced level of discernment to listen to certain records. You're too novice."

"What you mean? I can do it, I'm good."

"The type of vibration you send out will inevitably attract the kind of energy forces you will encounter in your life. The same goes for the kind of energy you choose to listen to," said the Chaplain.

"I know, I'll be fine. I picked this one for a reason. Synchronicity, right?"

The Chaplain quietly looks at X for a moment then takes a deep breath.

"Pick a number," says the Chaplain.

"5, every time," X replied with a smile.

The Chaplain places the record on the player and drops the needle on the vinyl. The beat dropped when the needle hit.

SCAN FOR MORE CONTENT AND TO UNLOCK ADDITIONAL CHAPTERS

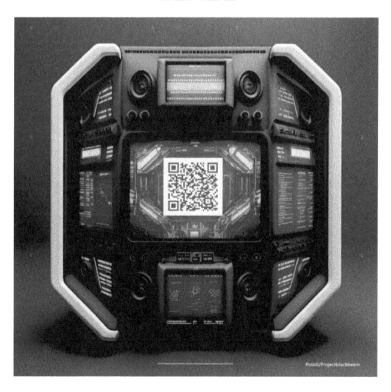

Even if the needle did just happen to fall that one time, he had still never witnessed someone catch on to a song so fast. The Chaplain lifted the needle. The record stopped and the lights returned to normal.

"Get up!" commanded the Chaplain, "have you rapped before?"

"No sir, I told you it was forbidden."

"Rap!" commanded the Chaplain. "Right now!"

"I don't know how to rap."

"I told you everyone can rap, some just not as well as they'd like but everyone can rap. Come on, what you got?"

He knew if X succeeded, he had to have been the one blessed to carry the God tongue. X began to rap.

[X]
"Metal in my arms
I'm firearms
Ring the alarms
From the infantry
And I'm in the CORR
Getting stronger

…

Everyday
Working hard
Say it like I mean
Mean what I say
uhh"

"Stop."

The Chaplain took a deep breath and shook his head.

"I told you I couldn't rap."

"That's not it, nobody really raps too much better than that their first time freestyling honestly. We just need more time to work on your flows, I have a feeling you'll find them. It's imperative to begin to practice, you can do it aloud or in your head. Don't hold back and don't doubt yourself. Really concentrate on what you're gonna say before you say it. One, two. Kick, punch it's all in your mind. The more you concentrate the farther you can go in. And don't forget to have enthusiasm. Now try again."

[X]

"Brown skin
Fight to win
With the Chaplain
He told me try this again
I don't know what I'm doing
But Ima keep going
Yea, haha."

X laughed at himself.

"That's good. You were rhyming and had better timing, now you must practice keeping from declining. Think of yourself like a walking magnet. You've seen one of those before, right?"

"Yes sir, back when I was smaller at the camps."

"Ok, so imagine yourself as a magnet continuously pulling toward you what you say, feel, and think. That's how you must view yourself as you develop your ability."

"Like a magnet." X said to himself.

"The universe is vibration aware of itself…It's all around us. You can feel it. That includes you and I. Tap into it and channel it into your words…again."

[X]
"I just really wanna end the war
And be a warrior in the CORR"
—"Say that again," said the Chaplain.
[X]
"I just really wanna end the war
And be a warrior in the CORR"
— "Again. Keep repeating it," said the Chaplain.
[X]
"I just really wanna end the war
And be a warrior in the CORR
I just really wanna end the war
And be a warrior in the CORR"
The Chaplain began to beat box along with X.
"I just really wanna end the war
And be a warrior in the CORR
I just really wanna end the war
And be a warrior in the CORR
I just really wanna end the war
And be a warrior in the CORR"

"Stop. I love that," said the Chaplain.
X smiled and laughed.
"Again."

FORT EVERS...PRESENT DAY 2109

"Sir we've just got word back about one of the missing boys from the unit," says one of the army officers to the commander.

"Where's our boy?" he replies.

"We've got footage from Aerotech of him fighting alongside resistance leadership sir."

"That son of a bitch, where?" the commander replied.

"He was last spotted disabling Aerotech equipment in Nevada sir."

"Well send some units to the area to go disable his little narrow ass then."

"Yes sir!"

BACK AT NEW KARNAK...

"Practice aloud or in your head and make sure whatever you do you tell the truth. Don't try to be too much like anybody you hear. Be yourself, the key is to be enthusiastic and to unlock those chakras. That's the key to everything we're doing here, find time to practice at least an hour a day and we'll see where you are next week. You're dismissed," said the Chaplain.

X left out and met back up with the rest of the recruits.

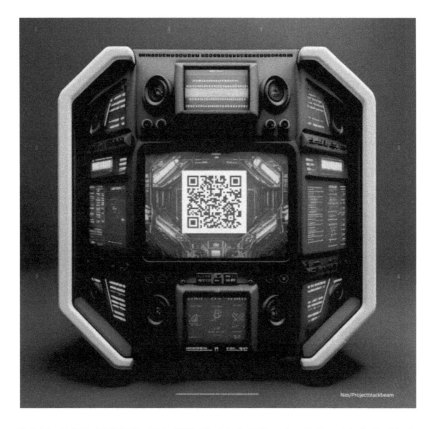

SCAN FOR MORE CONTENT AND TO UNLOCK ADDITIONAL
CHAPTERS

CHAPTER 1597

Machete and OG3 stand in front of the 5 neophytes as they squat on a wall beside a swimming pool. Each Neos' arms are stretched out in front of them as they each hold a plate covered in water. Their hands tremble with fatigue.

"The pain is in the mind, your imagination. Control your imagination and eliminate the pain," says Machete.

Some of the water from Jay Byrd's plate falls onto the decking.

"That's a fifteen-minute penalty. We gon be here all night," says OG3.

Some of the Neos' breathing gets heavier.

"Y'all can leave…y'all wanna drop?" asks Machete.

"Drip drop we never stop," the line replied in unison.

"Nah, go home. It's cool, bye," Machete responds.

None of the Neos move. OG3 goes down the line from the beginning.

"You wanna drop?"

"Drip drop we never stop!"

"You wanna drop?" he asks Bradley.

"Drip drop we never stop!" Bradley yells. OG3 continues down the line as they all respond the same.

"What's the key?" OG3 yells.

"Enthusiasm!" the line replies.

"What's the key?"

"Enthusiasm!"

"Y'all better keep this energy about you," said Machete. "It's the key to maintaining your Godly nature. The word enthusiasm comes from the Greek word enthousiasmos, meaning 'inspiration or possession by a God… Which you damn there better be."

A warrior enters the natatorium out of breath.

"Sir, a messenger from Amara just arrived. Says it's urgent."

"Bring the messenger," Machete replies.

The messenger is brought into the swimming hall in a hurry.

"Captain, Amara is under attack and is in danger of sustaining great loss."

The messenger handed Machete a device that displayed intelligence and footage of the battle taking place at Amara.

"Get the men ready!" yells Machete to OG3. "You two follow me, I'll relay your orders from the council," he says to the messenger and warrior.

They dart through the complex and into the King's chamber to share the news. He entered the quarters where the King sat listening to one of his ministers reading scripture from the King James Bible aloud.

"They know not, neither will they; understand; they walk on in darkness; all the foundations of the Earth are out of course. I have said, ye are'…,"

"Sire, we have news from Amara," announces Machete.

King Yahweh motions for the reading to stop.

"Enlighten me."

"They are under attack and are in danger of suffering great loss, your highness. I have ordered the men to ready their troops in case of invasion," said Machete as he handed King Yahweh the source of intelligence.

"Could this not have waited until the council met, Captain?"

"Sire."

"They are always under attack and in danger of suffering great loss. Continue to enact code orange, good day Captain," says King Yahweh.

Machete left King Yahweh's quarters to share the orders with the others. Equipped with mines and turrets the CORR was now made ready in case of invasion. A great silence had fallen on New Karnak as the fate of Amara was on everyone's minds. The colonies had seized communications through radio and other digital technology since the AI could hack into their systems and foil their operations. They were left to wait until messengers could deliver information between them.

X and a few others practiced rapping, beatboxing and calisthenics in the barracks. Loud explosions from fighting nearby began to shake the bay. Dust and sand fall from the ceiling with every boom.

"What's going on?" one of the recruits asked.

"They getting close," said Jay Byrd.

"I'm ready for whatever," said Destiny.

"You ready?" Bradley asked X.

X nodded his head yes. The explosions continued in the near distance.

Inside the train station warriors stood guard for the evening as a train approached New Karnak's station. The brakes scream and the doors open. Heather exited the train pulling a wounded warrior.

"Come on, he needs medical attention!" she yelled.

The warriors on the train platform rushed to her aid. The train was full of women, children, and wounded warriors.

"What happened?" One of the officers asked Heather.

"Close the hatches in the tunnel, we lost Amara!"

"What?" asks the Officer.

"Amara is gone! Close the Hatches!" she yells.

"Amara's gone, we lost Amara, we lost Amara!" the warriors yell out and repeat among each other. A sea of emotion floods the train station.

"Close the hatches!" the officer orders his men.

Machete accompanied by 4 armed warriors came to see what the disturbance was.

"Sir, we just got word we've lost Amara," one of the warriors in the station says to Machete.

"No! Any officers present?" Machete asks.

"She's right over there," the warrior replied as he pointed to Heather.

Machete walked over to Heather. Her shirt stained with blood.

"Tell me we didn't lose Amara," he says to her. She shook her head no.

"It's gone," she says with tears in her eyes.

Machete got down on one knee and pinched the bridge of his nose to compose himself and hold back his tears.

"We have to deliver Scarab to stop them. We don't have much time," Heather cries.

"That's right…defeat the AI…You, have it? It's finished?"

"Yes, I managed to escape with the others before the republic's forces could Rupture the barricade to the train station."

Machete stood back up.

"How do we use it?"

"We need to insert the software directly into the computer's mainframe."

"Like into one of the Mechs walking around out there?"

"No…I wish it were that easy. Before we were overrun, we located the AI's mainframe. It's orbiting Earth, operating the Mechs remotely."

"That's how they keep it safe. The only ships are at Amara."

"They may have already been destroyed by now," said Heather.

"Understood, It's our only shot. We gotta try," Machete replied.

King Yahweh got the news of Amara and called an emergency meeting with his council and high-ranking officers.

"We must leave now," Princess Leone cautions.

"Enemy forces are already directly above us. How can we leave?" asks Curtis.

"We don't have a choice!" said another council member.

"Silence! We meet them before they get to us. They won't expect us to be in an offensive position. Besides, they've already brought the fight to Amara, so we keep them there," said King Yahweh.

"Your majesty, with all due respect Code orange and red are rendered ineffective if we send forces to retake Amara," Machete replies.

An explosion is heard in the distance. The room rumbles and the lights flicker.

"We will not sit idle in obscurity while Amara is burning to the ground, Captain! You will ready companies A and B for deployment and suit up the recruits to defend the temple," the King replied.

Machete replies sharply, "No, we do not have the numbers to split the units effectively. We can only spare maybe a squad. We have possession of Scarab. It's ready to be deployed. A small unit can go undetected and take a ship from Amara and…,"

"Watch yourself Captain," said one of the advisors.

"The most certain route to victory is by delivering Scarab sire," Machete pleads.

"You will do what I have told you, Captain," King Yahweh replies.

"And let you turn this place to ruins? No, that I cannot do," Machete stands to leave and carry out his plans.

"Seize him!" orders the King.

The King's Guards shoot Machete with tasers. He struggles for a moment but then rips the two electric prongs from his body. 3 other guards enter the chamber and hit him with shots of electricity that surge through his body and bring him to his knees. They remove him from the chamber. OG3 was the next officer in the chain of command and assumed Machete's role.

"You will lead the men to Amara and equip the recruits to defend the temple walls," said the King to OG3.

"As you wish, sire," replied OG3 as he glowered at the King with discontent.

MEANWHILE IN THE BARRACKS BAY...

More explosions can be heard in the distance that send vibrations through the room. A red light begins to flash and turns everything in the room red. The recruits spill out of the bay and into the quad where there are hundreds of people gathered. There were warriors, engineers, shop keepers, doctors, and children. A moment of silence was dedicated to the lives lost at Amara.

●●●

A warrior standing atop a large staircase speaks for all to hear. "Alpha company and Beta company have orders to travel to Amara and retake the colony!"

People in the crowd gasp.

"Charlie company will stay here and defend the temple walls! We leave for Amara in 30 minutes! All citizens, Nobles, and council are to seek refuge within the temple walls!"

"It's time bro," Rodney says to X.

"Let's do it," X replied.

"Must've gotten pretty ugly at Amara if they sending two companies to retake it," Rodney replies.

Some of the warriors huddle together to ceremonially drink from a chalice and to rap and recite affirmations in a cipher as they often do in preparation for battle.

"My blood and homeland on the line,
Got protection from the most high so I know we fine
Full of light and of love so they can't stop the shine
Through the darkness and pain always kept piece of mind,
We gon Fight for this shit we ain't finna let up
Think they fuckin wit us that aint how it's set up
Heard they coming for us load the howitzers up
Magazines full of rounds hold a thousand and up
Fear in our hearts never knew how that felt
Upper wards a get news how they came through and fell
They want war cuz they whores and they don't know they self
Man we already won, claim this shit with yall mouth."

OG3 met the recruits and Neos back at the barracks bay.

"Everybody don your gear and gather in the Armory!" he says.

"We going on the front line huh?" asks Bradley.

"Yeah, y'all can consider yourselves members of the CORR now, congratulations," said OG3.

"Sorry we couldn't cross y'all the traditional way yet but that's what happens when you let someone who ain't made run the ship. We'll take care of that once this is all over. They don't understand the significance of certain shit."

There were over 200 Mechs traveling from Amara and surrounding the areas above the temple and nearly a battalion of military soldiers including a few companies of mechanized youth soldiers. Resistance fighters set off fire bombs and mines to slow down the advance of enemy forces and to thwart artillery unit's attacks. As the night progressed, fire fights between resistance warriors and military forces broke out closer to the temple location. Alpha and Beta company deployed earlier to head off enemy forces and retake Amara. X and the new recruits now patrolled the temple walls protecting the clergy and the citizens of New Karnak.

Heather waited until the blunt of CORR forces vacated the temple walls to locate Machete. Sanctorium floats above Heather's head as it scans the cell Machete was in and disengages the lock.

"Come on, we can't have you sitting around here like some bum," Heather says.

Machete exited the cell and smiled.

"Most of the forces have left, it's mostly just recruits left," she says.

"Let's go. King Yahweh is a fool and will pay for his incompetence," Machete declares.

They darted through the complex and on their way out, Heather noticed X and the other 4 Neos pulling guard at one of the hatches with a group of other warriors.

"X!" she called out.

He looked to see who it was and saw Heather and Machete.

"Heather! Captain!" X called out.

"What are you doing here? Are you alright?"

"Amara is gone X."

X shook his head, "I'm sorry."

"We fought but were overrun. There was just too many," Heather cries.

"What about Heka?"

Heather shook her head no. Her eyes rim with tears. X lowers his head.

"We need to destroy the AI controlling the Mechs. We don't have any more time to spare. You 3 come with us," Machete says to X, Rodney, and Jay Byrd.

"Yes sir," they reply.

"You 2 stay here, the warriors here are gonna need you. Lead them to victory," says Machete to the others.

"Ya'll gonna be good here? We're gonna take care of this AI before they can swarm this place," says X.

Bradley Nods and says, "We good, yall just come back in one piece."

"Too easy," said Destiny.

The two groups part ways.

"The software...it's at Amara?" asked X.

"No, I have it. We had just finished developing the code before the Mechs attacked and forced their way inside. Amara is our only hope to get it to the mainframe in time," she says as they sprint through the complex.

"It's orbiting space and our ships are at Amara."

"Like a satellite?"

"Yeah, we can take one of the planes here back to Amara to see if there are any ships still there, that's our best bet."

"What if they gone?" Jay Byrd asks.

"We lose," said Machete as he types on a LED screen next to a bay door holding the planes inside.

"We keep Falcon 8's for emergency evacuations. The rail launch should get us out of here without taking on too much heat," Machete assures.

Everyone boards the Falcon 8 and take off uncontested to Amara.

-- --

"The AI is embedded within the satellite of a private communication company's network called 'Star-connect'. It's not military, it's just a space station so we should be able to get inside without too much resistance," says Heather.

"Star-connect? They hid it in plain sight. You don't think that AI is gonna see us coming?" asks Machete.

"Star-connect?" asks X.

"We don't have any other option, and yes," Heather replied.

"Wait, Star-connect stored ships in hangers at Fort Evers. Said it was for maintenance or something," explains X.

"Yeah?" asks Machete.

"How do we even know it's any ships left at Amara?" X asks.

"We don't," Heather replies.

"Let's just take one of the ships from Fort Evers, we got a better chance at the AI not getting any ideas like that, right?" asked X.

"Them circuits must be frying in ya motherboard right now cuz what?" said Jay Byrd.

"We don't have enough time to go just to find out there's nothing left of Amara," says X.

"He might be right," Machete said in agreement.

"How do you suppose we get our hands on a heavily guarded ship and fly it outta there?" asks Jay Byrd.

"They didn't guard the Star-connect ships like they did the fighter jets when I was there. We just need to keep a low profile. Most of the security is at the entrance and near the armory. It's easier to get on base than it looks. A Lot easier than sneaking off," X replies.

"A distraction," said Heather.

"Most of the AI's combat units are probably farther north right now anyway. This could be our only chance," Machete added.

A loud rumbling can be heard in the distance.

"You hear that?" asks Heather.

"Yeah, bad news," Machete replied.

2 fighter jets approach and maintain a close distance at the altitude of the falcon's wings. A voice is heard over the radio in the cockpit.

"This is the U.S. Air Force, you have been intercepted. If you've received this transmission, acknowledge the radio call and rock your wings."

"Bruh, we can take 'em right?" asks Jay Byrd.

"I got a plan," says Machete.

"I repeat, acknowledge the call and rock your wings."

"What are we gonna do?" asks Heather.

One of the jets crosses right across the Falcon 8's nose.

"Follow or you will be shot down," said the voice from the radio.

"X get ready," says Machete as he pulls back the thruster, increasing the speed driving directly behind the Jet that passed. He opens fire taking it out. The other jet begins to fire on the falcon 8 as Machete does a barrel roll and several maneuvers in an attempt to evade. Machete tried to find a firing position but was unsuccessful. The Jet fighter followed with incessant firing. The plane shook whenever they took a hit.

"I'm gonna open the cargo ramp, X take them out!" orders Machete as he takes the plane completely vertical.

The jet follows behind him straight into the air as Machete releases a smoke screen countermeasure. X charges his man cannon and grabs hold of a pole as the cargo ramp opens. The Fighter jet clears the smoke and X fires a beam straight through it's cockpit. The shot creates an implosion and the fighter jet slowly falls from the sky.

BACK AT NEW KARNAK MOMENTS EARLIER...

"Sire, Captain Machete escaped. He's taken one of the Falcons," said one of the King's guards.

The King didn't respond.

"Sire…," he said.

"I heard you," the King replied.

Loud explosions and nearby gun fire ring out and shake the complex. Another warrior runs into the room.

"Sire enemy forces have breached the wall!" he said.

"Sire, what do you want us to do?" the other soldier asks.

"Defend the walls!" says the King.

The King grabs his armor and rifle.

"Go!" he yells.

He and his guards head toward the fighting. Melanated mechanized soldiers and roamers enter the palace walls firing indiscriminately.

"In the midst of chaos, there is also opportunity"
-Sun-Tzu, The Art of war

CHAPTER 2584

X AND THE OTHERS MAKE IT TO FORT EVERS...

"You sure that's it?" asks Heather as they stooped next to the gate nearest the airfield.

"That's Star-connect's hangar," X replies.

"Pretty unguarded like you said. We need to hurry," says Jay Byrd.

"I'll take care of causing a distraction big enough for y'all to get in the air, Jaleel and Rodney on me. You two get to that satellite, we'll be sure to grab you when you touch back down. They're gonna be pretty pissed off so be ready to come in hot. And ayy...welcome to the CORR gentlemen," says Machete before he and the others dart off into the darkness.

Heather programs Sanctorium from a device on her forearm to begin scanning the area and for it to prepare to assist her with piloting the ship. After a few moments a loud explosion and mushroom cloud of fire that turned into black smoke appeared a half mile away from where they were. A drone patrolling the grounds nearby flew in the direction of the blast.

"That's our cue," says X.

He shot a charge from his arm that put a hole big enough for them to fit through in the gate.

"After you," he said.

He and Heather sprint through the airfield and into the hangar. A fleet of parked Star-connect shuttles awaited them.

"Let's fuckin Go!" yells X in excitement.

Heather laughed. Sanctorium flew through the hangar scanning the vehicles for the most mission ready craft.

"We got one," yells Heather.

The flying chrome ball Sanctorium remotely opened the doors and started the ship. They board. The ship rolled out the hangar, gained speed on the runway and took off. It shot through the atmosphere. Sanctorium plays "Pyramid" by ALYSS while securing itself in Heather's lap. X and Heather's hands meet over the arm rests...

MEANWHILE BACK AT NEW KARNAK...

King Yahweh watches from a balcony as the Chaplain fights against several soldiers who enter the temple all on his own. The Chaplain uses his mouth to beatbox a rhythm only he hears. He is one of the few members of the CORR that has mastered manipulating sounds into rhythms that can provide him a slight edge in battle. An ascended beatboxer can manipulate sounds in a room to repeat at will, creating elaborate compositions that cause an altering of the virtual space and of the otherwise naturally occuring rhythm in a room.

For the enemy it's like being a seasoned professional quarterback dropping back and stepping up into a pocket to throw but his rhythm is unexpectedly off. The timing of every drop back that quarterback ever experienced has helped ingrain memory into his muscles but with a beat boxer on defense that quarterback is in trouble.

The steps, the breathing, reads and release are now out of sync. Now imagine this same effect in battle. This is why our ancestors played drums and instruments in battle. To sway the rhythms and vibrations in their favor. The Chaplain fights with speed, grace, and poise. Using soldiers as cover and delivering debilitating blows that land in sync with his rhythm. 7 soldiers attack and they can't get a steady hand nor a shot at him.

"Sir, forces are entering from the west wing," says a warrior to King Yahweh. Roamers and mechanized soldiers fire in King Yahweh's direction. He watches from behind cover as turret fire rips a few of his fighters to bits.

He then runs and takes cover behind the security hatch doors line. He looks back to see his men running to join him in safety as Mechs march and assault behind them. He closes the hatch before any of them can make it.

THE SHUTTLE LEAVES EARTH...

"There it is...," says Heather.

"Docking...autopilot engaged," said a droid's voice from the ship.

The ship connected to the satellite and was guided into the bay as the airlock decompressed.

"The mainframe's here somewhere," said Heather as she analyzes the ship's layout with a device that projects a 3 dimensional map over her right forearm.

They walk through several rooms in the satellite. It was like a football stadium filled with servers.

"Right through here," said Heather as they walked into a room that resembled a cockpit. Heather reached into one of her pockets and grabbed the Scarab program. Sanctorium projected the encryption and code.

Heather uses this to guide her through the process of infiltrating the A.I. X watches as she opens a fuse box and cuts chords. An alarm begins to go off in the cockpit.

"It's alright, I got it," says Heather.

The alarm blared for a few seconds and stopped once she situated the Scarab device in the fuse box.

"That's it?" X asks.

"Yea, just needs to filter through the system. It looks a little different up here than we projected…but hey, y'all are gonna have a big ass crossing ceremony when we get back. Shits gonna be bananas!" she says with a smile.

"Yea, we actually made it."

"Second LT X. It's got a little ring to it."

They both share a chuckle.

A few minutes pass as the program loads.

"Ay I think we got company," says X.

A ship approached the dock.

"Caution. Ship Docking," said the android's voice from within the cockpit's system.

"I'll seal us in here. Should buy us enough time until the bug overrides the encryption," Heather declares.

Heather radios to Machete from the cockpit.

"Captain, come in!"

"Glad to hear you made it. Tell me some good news! We're ready for our Rendezvous," he replies.

On the monitors in the cockpit, they could see the enemy ship's crew of soldiers disabling the ship X and Heather had used to travel. Heather and X shared a gaze and a moment of silence.

"We'll be fine," says X.

"We've got company up here, sir."

"You got company up there, we got company down here. They're still tracking our comms!" says Machete.

A crew of soldiers clear the satellite looking for intruders then finally attempt to enter the cockpit. Heather hacked the program to seal the doors from the inside. The soldiers use a walker to begin cutting through the doors.

"Come on, it should've been done by now," says Heather.

"They're almost through the doors."

"It's the firewall for the AI, it's adapting to the code. I'll do what I can to cripple it manually. If they get through you gotta hold them off!" Heather says as she begins to enter data into the control panel of the cockpit.

"You got it!"

X began to charge the man cannon in his arm and aim it at the door.

"What are you doing? You can't use that thing in here."

X powered it down and positioned himself to get a jump on whoever came through the door.

The cutting stops. The door is kicked open. The soldiers fire rounds into the room. X grabs the lead soldier's weapon and wrist. The soldier shot into the air as they struggled. Steam burst from the pipes on the ceiling. X crushes the wrist of the soldier he grabs and throws him into another soldier.

The last soldier shoots at X's head at close range but X was able to clear his head of the soldier's line of fire. X delivers a 3-punch combination that ends with a gut punch strong enough to break the soldier's back. One of the men reaches for the weapon on the floor. X kicks it and kicks the soldier knocking him unconscious as his body slides across the floor.

The first soldier moans on the floor holding his crushed wrist. X picks up the weapon that was kicked and shoots him with it. X goes back into the cabin to see Heather on the floor with her hands covered in blood as she holds her stomach. She had been shot through her side.

"Heather!" X runs over to put pressure on her wound.

"No...we gotta get you back down to Earth," he says as he sat beind her on the floor and positioned himself to apply pressure to her wound.

"I'll be ok," she whispers.

"Tell me what to do. How do we finish this thing?" X asks in a panicked tone.

"It's nothing we can do...the encryption...look," she replies.

Bullets had traveled into parts of the panel and control boards of the cockpit.

"It's gotta be another way."

Heather shook her head no.

"Warning airlock disengaged," says a droid's voice from the radio system. The pilot inside the enemy's spacecraft had left his men to retreat to Earth. X's eyes pace the room as he goes deep into his mind for the answer.

"We have to destroy this ship...we don't have any more time," says X.

"You're right," Heather replies, "but if we go back to Earth... they'll swarm our location...and take it before we can act."

Gunfire can be heard from Machete by transmission.

"It can't end like this."

X could feel his heartbeat pounding in his ears. He thinks back to the others waiting for them to come back to Earth and all the people being attacked back at the temple. He thinks about everyone back at Amara who had died. He reminisces about Heka and Heka's mother. He thinks about his own mother. About Heather and how dedicated they both were to the CORR. Everything he learned about his life and his purpose. Everyone was fighting selflessly to the death just for a chance to live a life they believed in. Suddenly the truth of his next statement dawns on him...

"We may not get the choice to be brought in this world...but we can choose what's really worth leaving it for," says X under his breath.

"Hmm?" asks Heather.

He takes a deep breath and lets it out. He feels his fear of death leave his body like a guest after a pleasant visit in his home.

"It's something I heard Heka say…What if we just flew it out of range?"

"Out of range?"

"Yeah, like away from the Mechs on Earth…It's remote. It's gotta have a max range, maybe we can reach it."

Heather thought to herself for a moment, "you're right. We can give it a try, but we'd have to stay out here. We'll just be...oh," she says as she paused to lock eyes with X.

X interlocks his hand around hers.

— *"No...just come back on the shuttle. What're you talking about…"* says Machete through the transmission.

"The shuttle is inoperable. Amara is gone…the research is gone," she shakes her head.

— *"Just wait, we can figure something out,"* says Machete concerned. Continuous machine gun fire from the Mechs can be heard from over the comms.

"Let's do it," Heather says as she coughs. They won't let us get another chance. Our people don't have any more time."

MEANWHILE ON EARTH...

Machete, Rodney, and Jay Byrd hold out in a storage building on base under heavy fire from Mech and drone units who cornered them there.

"We can't stay here. They're gonna bring the whole block down on us!" says Jay Byrd.

"We hold here till we know where these two are gonna land!" orders Machete. Shell casings clink and clank as they pile up at the feet of the Mechs. Turret fire keep Machete and the others pinned to the floor.

"Come on you 2!" says Machete to himself as he looks up to the sky through a window.

"We pissed em off pretty bad down here," says Jay Byrd.

"We ain't leaving here without you 2! You hear me? Send those grids! That's an order!" orders Machete.

"Ahhhh!" yells Jay Byrd as pieces of the building begin to collapse around them.

A distorted illegible message came over Machete's comm system.

"Say again! Your landing grids now!" Machete orders.

"Look!" says Jay Byrd.

A streak of light trailed above the horizon. The Mech seized fire and stood still…